To David,

with good wishes

thank

[signature]

Alfredo Hunter: the Man With the Pen.

Alfredo Hunter:
the Man
With the Pen.

by

Chris Sullivan

Library of Congress Cataloging-in-Publication Data

Sullivan, Chris
   Alfredo Hunter: the Man With the Pen.

Copyright © 2009 by Chris Sullivan

ALL RIGHTS RESERVED. No part of this book may be
reproduced in any manner with the express written content
of the publisher, except in the case of brief excerpts in critical
reviews and articles. All inquiries should be addressed to:
JMP, Post Office Box 931405, Los Angeles, California, 90093.

Printed in the United States of America.

This story is dedicated to you – the reader . .

Prologue

The Man with the Pen

Once upon a time, and a long time ago
It was, in the city of Dublin,
In the land of Ireland, there was a man
With a pen; and this man with the pen gave it
To a little fella who wrote many
A poem, limerick and story;
And the poems, limericks and stories
Spread to the four corners of the world, it was a square world;
And the poems, limericks and stories
That spread to the four corners of the world
Made the earth round - into a great ball -
'Surrounded by clouds' as the great man once said!

Near the ball there was a moon, which added
Romance and imagination to the poems,
Limericks and stories; and around all this
Were stars and planets and they formed a system
Called the solar system;
And it was solar and alone;
And writers came along and looked to the moon,
And beyond, to the stars and planets
In the solar system for inspiration:
And when they got the inspiration they needed
They used the pen to write; for that is what a pen is for.

And the man with the pen looked down at the writers,
Whenever they were in their blocks,
And gave them the start that they needed
And this is how the writers of Ireland
Told the people of the world the absolute truth –
Which they had found on the wall
Of Bewley's Coffee shop in Grafton Street Dublin;
For there were many in Bewley's would put the world to right
In an afternoon's confabulation.

But the writer was always the little fella;
The little fella who had to meet the big bad bullies
When he was at school; the big bad bullies
That made him take part
In their big bad bumpy games,
Which would frighten the poor little fella,
At that very early and tender age
When all the boys had to learn to head the greasy leather orb
Which they called a football;
Had to go into that big bad world
Which they called a school;
Had to find out that most of the bullies
Were the teachers: teachers who took great pleasure
And unnatural delight
In striking many a young child across the backside
With their canes and slippers;
But the little writer would get his own back
On the big bad bullies for he would write about them.

Sometimes, but not often, the big bad bully

Would read what the little writer had written

And knock the be Jesus out of him;

Break his glasses,

Knock the pen out of the little fella's hand

And burn his books:

At four hundred and fifty one degrees Fahrenheit.

But there was always somebody

To pick up that pen and look up,

Up towards the stars in the heaven

Where they would seek the same stimulation;

And the man with the pen would look down and give it.

****

1

One of the writers who looked up to stars in the heaven was my friend Alfredo.

The first time I saw Alfredo was in Highland Avenue, Hollywood; it was a January evening just before darkness; the weather in January can be hot during the Los Angeles day and cold when the sun goes down; it was a coldish evening but not cold enough for breath vapour; in fact I don't think that has ever happened in Los Angeles even though I have heard rumours to the contrary.

Alfredo was walking towards me as I walked north away from Hollywood Boulevard going to my part time evening job in the Cahuenga Pass. He ambled along like a prize-fighter and looked fairly muscular but when I got closer I could see that he was overweight around the belly area; then he stopped walking.

"God-damn," he said, softly, punching his fist lightly into the air; and then he turned round and walked back up the hill and in to a seedy hotel.

The seedy hotel usually smelled of shit, if it rained, and I had seen some very peculiar people coming and going as I passed every day.

Later that evening, around nine-thirty, Alfredo came out of the seedy hotel again, just after I passed it on my way home, and walked in the same direction, down the hill towards Hollywood Boulevard walking a couple of yards behind. When I walked a little faster he walked a little faster. We walked like that for about twenty yards or so and it was becoming unnerving; what was he doing? I turned and called over my shoulder "How's it going?"

"Hey man," he said, "you took the words out of my mouth – how you doing?"

Did I grunt something? I don't know but we walked side-by-side down towards Hollywood: me going back to my digs in Silverlake and he….

"Hey man," he said, "I just got out of the penitentiary. I'm in that hotel and I ain't got no choice man!"

"You got the wrong man here," I said, "I'm broke."

I looked at him and it seemed as if he was in a trance.

"That's why I'm walking!" I added.

"No," he said, "I don't want your money. I gotta go and buy something to eat at a shitty café."

This time his accent had changed.

"What part of Dublin are you from?" I asked.

"The south side; you?"

"Ballybough."

The north side.

"So what's with the Yankee accent?"

"Ah, you know" he said 'just trying to fit in."

He had no green card and no work permit of any kind and had entered the country through Canada so how could he have been in the penitentiary, as he put it? I think he just liked saying the word penitentiary instead of using gaol or prison.

Over the next week or so we met quite a few times on my trek from work each day and we talked as we walked. At Hollywood Boulevard I would cross over, and wait for the bus to Silverlake, which stopped outside the MacDonald's and the Ripley's 'Believe it or Not Museum,' and he would turn right to go to his shitty café.

One night as I waited for the bus with the hookers, druggies, down and outs and other members of the vagrant train, who invariably hung around that corner, I'm sure I felt him staring at my back so when I turned round I wasn't surprised when I saw him standing on the corner of Highland and Hollywood looking over at me. It was a distance of about fifty yards or so but I could easily recognize his shape; he seemed to have an intense gaze and a slight stoop forward, which transmitted all of that distance. I acknowledged him then he waved and walked on. He must have been standing there looking at me for many minutes before I noticed!

"How'd you get your green card?" he asked one day.

"The lottery."

"Ah you won the lottery! How'd that go?"

"Write your name on a piece of paper, prove you're Irish and send it off to an address in Virginia, somewhere. I'll get the details for you."

"I don't want you to do that. I don't want a job."

Then he stopped in the street.

"I don't want a fucking job," he said, "I'm here to make a killing."

"A killing?"

"Yeh; I have to make a killing."

Alfredo was a brilliant playwright, so he said, and I tended to believe him, and his plays had been produced in San Francisco, Marin County and Canada. He was commissioned to write a play, one time, by a movie star who promptly died just after he had started the first draft. He wouldn't tell me who the movie star was.

"Rock Hudson?"

"Feck off! It was my chance to have something on Broadway and it'll never happen again."

"How do you know?"

"It'll never happen again!"

"Where's the play now."

He tapped the purse on his belt then tapped his head and we walked on.

I looked forward to our tête-à-tête each day; I could finish work any time I wanted as there were no fixed hours but I usually stayed till the company closed, which was nine-o-clock. I called people in their homes to try and sell tickets for the Hollywood Bowl or for concerts to The Los Angeles Philharmonic Orchestra. Sounds easy enough and it would have been if it was to sell tickets for Rod Stewart or even a single ticket to a concert but the job was to sell a series of tickets to classical concerts. It was mind destroying and I often wondered what I was doing in Los Angeles. Was it to make a killing like Alfredo?

I had to work at telemarketing and I knew I didn't have any choice if I wanted to stay in Los Angeles unless to work in a bar or restaurant where I had no experience. What kind of chance would I stand? I didn't know what I wanted to do. I could see thousands of actors after too few jobs and I could see writers of Alfredo's supposedly immense talent trying to sell shitty screenplays to the film and television world. He was probably capable of writing the great Irish novel but he wanted to make a killing.

You may ask yourself why an Irishman would be called Alfredo; I never did find out why he wanted to sound Italian or Spanish - I just figured that if he wanted to sound exotic that was up to him. He also used American spelling in the writing of his screenplays. I would have thought that it would be better to write as an Irishman but he said that it wasn't and that if ever anybody was interested in his work he said he would never meet them:

"They're ageist too," he would say.

Did I make a mistake by telling him a room was available in the house where I was staying? I don't know! But living with Alfredo was certainly some kind of very rich experience.

He told me he had fallen out with the last old witch of a landlady and he had to leave a lot of his stuff there when he left, as she wouldn't let him back into the house. He said he had to send his friend, Milton, who moved his worldly goods into a storage unit in Silverlake for him.

"That's convenient." I said, "The house is in Silverlake."

I was sharing the house with two others: a retired realtor from Florida and an actress called Betty who had been a regular character in a Los Angeles soap opera. The fella was also in Los Angeles to make a killing and was probably close to seventy. However he looked younger than Alfredo whose age I couldn't even guess. Patrick was going through a divorce and just starting out as an actor. The fact that he couldn't act and had no experience of it didn't faze him one little bit. His girl friends had told him he was good looking enough to go to Hollywood to get into a series and that's why he came. A different kind of killing from the one Alfredo was after but a killing nonetheless.

He was doing the crossword in the newspaper one day and said: "Name one of Lear's daughters. Who's Lear?"

So he was all set with his ignorance, his 'no talent' and his sun tan for Hollywood. I think Betty, the soap opera queen, wasn't very impressed with his talent or intelligence, but she could see that he was a man who got up early every morning, went for a long walk, came back and cooked his breakfast and then took a shower and got on with his day. In other words he functioned so she could be sure that the garbage would be wheeled out every Thursday come rain or shine. He was also a Roman Catholic and went to the Catholic Church across the street every Sunday; but he wouldn't sit with the Latinos, which was a bit difficult in a predominantly Mexican area.

He kept trying to get me to go to church with him "Come on," he would say, "in case there is a God."

In case there is a God!

On the other hand Alfredo couldn't do anything apart from write. Oh he could play the guitar and the banjo; and he could understand Yung and Freud was very fond of James Joyce and Arthur Koestler; he knew who King Lear was and that he had three daughters; was widely read and was very interested in politics, psychoanalysis, schizophrenia, psychology and a lot of other 'ologies.' He was also manic-depressive or bi-polar as they got to say, which I didn't know until he moved in.

The situation at the house suited me; I liked the fact that Betty and Patrick were a lot older than me and they kind of treated me like they were my parents; I had lived in a house with some young people before and I didn't like it.

Before I came to live in Los Angeles I was wary of the fact that people carried guns: the cops, the security guards at the supermarkets and mini-malls carry guns and all the drug dealers on every street corner have a piece just in case a deal goes wrong or they have to shoot it out with the police; especially if the whole place is stinking with cops, they are surrounded and there is no way out. I'm happy to say that things are not like that at all; the cops and security guards yes but other than that, seeing an incident with a gun is about as common as seeing a road accident in Ireland: they do happen, you hear about them but by the time you get there it's all over bar the shouting and you see a lot more road accidents than gun incidents.

I saw my first none cop gun within a couple of weeks of arriving. For some reason the first place I lived here was in a city called Sylmar which is about twenty miles north of Los Angeles near San Fernando; a friend of a friend knew a Deejay who knew someone who knew an Englishman with a room to let in a house.

Sylmar was just a name to me; it was famous for the 1971 earthquake but that's about all so when I agreed to stay there I didn't know it was so far away and that I had to travel on five – yes five freeways: adding to the risk of the freeways, to this stranger to driving on the right hand side of the road for the first time, was the fact that it was the rainy season and when it rains in Southern California it really rains; it rains so hard that the drains can't take the water away fast enough so the trucks, aquaplaning their way up north to Sacramento and San Francisco, would send such huge spurts and sprays of water all over my windscreen that more than once I thought my end had come and I was about to meet my maker.

Getting off the last freeway and landing in Sylmar, and it was like landing, was like landing in the Pacific Ocean after a space flight – tranquility.

Sylmar is a city where the first thing you see, after the Motel 6, is a very wide street where, it is said, young kids race cars in the wee small hours of the morning; in fact you think about the movie 'American Graffiti.'

The Englishman, who owned the house, turned out to be a young fella from the Channel Islands; I had replaced a Texan who had gone to live in a trailer park in the San Fernando Valley. The Texan came back for a visit, one evening, and as we sat talking it was quite obvious that he hadn't got on too well with his erstwhile landlord as he was talking disparagingly about him over a beer in the living room. He also told me about his trailer and how cheap it was to live there. I asked him how dangerous it was: "I always have a gun under my pillow" he said.

With that he stood up with a swagger and took a chrome pistol from inside his jacket and started swinging it about: "Look!" he said "It's got a full metal jacket . ."

I put my hand up "Hang on a minute!" I said.

"Typical Limey" he said "scared o' guns."

"I just don't like them when they're pointed at me;" I said "and by the way - I'm Irish."

"Y'all sound the same to me;" he said.

As I said that the Channel Islander came back from his room to see the Texan standing in the middle of the floor waving his gun as if he was Alan Ladd looking for Jack Palance "What are you doing here?" he said nastily.

"Visiting" said Tex.

He was actually waiting for the other man sharing the house who was in the bathroom.

"I've told you before about beer on the carpet" said the Channel Islander "use the bloody table or a coaster."

Then he disappeared into the kitchen: "He's an asshole;" said the Texan "sits in his room all night jerking off."

The 'jerking off' bit was said in a raised voice so that the Channel Islander could hear and it wasn't hard to guess why the Texan had left the confines of the house in Sylmar for the wilds of the San Fernando Valley.

"How do you get on with him?" He said.

"Okay."

I wasn't particularly fond of the Channel Islander but that was because I hardly knew him as he kept himself to himself in his room doing whatever he did in there; he had let me stay in the house without any money changing hands, as I didn't have any, and believed me when I said I would pay him when I got paid from my job that I had just started the week before.

The Channel Islander came back from the kitchen carrying a drink and went straight into his room cocking the Texan a snooty look as he passed; the Texan gave the finger to his back.

"A lot of us carry guns" he said "we were out last week in a restaurant and on our table four out of the five of us there were carrying a piece."
Wow a piece! We were really in the vernacular of the place, I thought.

"When do you shoot it?" I said.

"We go out into the desert at night and shoot – we're going tonight; wanna come?"

"No thanks." I said.

He shrugged as his Columbian friend came into the room; it has to be said they didn't look particularly dressed to go shooting. The Texan put the gun back into his pocket: "Let's go." He said.

They went towards the door and the Columbian turned to me "I got a good movie to watch tomorrow night; Natural Born Killers!"

"Great" I said and the two armed men walked out the front door.

For the brief time I lived there I had a rental car and as that was the only way to get there I needed to get a place near to where I was working and that's when I found Betty's house.

On the day Alfredo came to meet us at the house we were sitting around the dining room table. The house had been in a glum mood for a week as a bomb had gone off in Oklahoma killing hundreds of people. Patrick had amended his racist language since the bombing, as he said he didn't want his comments to cause harm. It was only a temporary situation, however, as he polluted the air with his usual racist epithets as soon as the Oklahoma bombing went out of his head.

When Alfredo came in through the front door he greeted us with a huge smile. He hadn't bothered to comb his wild mass of white hair and looked as if he had just been in a war. I still don't know what impression he wanted to make. Maybe he thought it made him look arty or intellectual!

I introduced them: "This is Betty," I said, "and this is Patrick."

He kept hold of Patrick's hand as he looked him in the eye and repeated:

"Patrick ….. Patrick."

Later on I asked him why he did that: "When I came in I saw a good looking guy sitting there at the table," he said; "well two good looking guys if I count you:" he laughed at that. "Then when I looked at him" he continued "I could see how vain he was and vanity is one of the ugliest of ugly things and he got uglier the more I looked at him."

"Well Betty!" I said, "Are you going to show him the room?"

"Yes," she said, and almost jumped out of her seat.

"Didn't tell me he was a Jew," said Patrick, when they had both disappeared.

"I didn't notice," was my reply. And I hadn't! "Does it make any difference?"

"Not to me," said Patrick.

Patrick was a strange man to try and understand. He was the opposite of Betty. She was a Democrat and he was a Republican. He was the only American I ever met who was proud of the McCarthy witch-hunts of the fifties. He was Irish-American but hated the Kennedys both dead and alive. My first impression was that he was too dim to be anything but harmless but his dimness and lack of tact seemed to do more harm than good and all he was really good for was putting the garbage out each Thursday.

The room Betty was showing Alfredo was at the front of the house on the ground floor. It would give him a view of life going on outside whilst he worked. It had a bunk bed; I wasn't sure if Alfredo would like it like that but when he came out with Betty he was looking very pleased with himself.

"I'll be able to have my lap-top underneath me whilst I sleep and when I get up in the mornings I'll be at work straight away."

Betty told him that he would have to share the bathroom with me as I was on the ground floor too; at the back with a view of the garden. She told him that there was a phone line in his room and that he was welcome to use her telephone, which was next to her as she spoke, till he had his own line activated.

"Okay," he said, "I'll take it."

"I don't know about that," said Betty, "I think we need to discuss. . . ."

Then she referred to Patrick and me: "Between the three of us," she added.

"Betwixt and between!" he chuckled, "Okay! I'll go outside for five minutes. Should be enough time for you?"

I looked at the other two and they seemed to be in a state of shock.

"Okay by me," I said, and he turned to go.

"I'll be back in five minutes," he said as he walked out.

"What's his last name?" asked Patrick

"I don't know," I said.

"Hunter," said Betty, "he just told me. Wanted to know if I minded Jews and I told him I welcomed them!"

She said this provocatively to Patrick.

"You said what?" said Patrick.

"Don't you like Jews?" I asked

"They don't worry me," he said then he paused and looked at Betty: "they don't worry me."

"Is Hunter a Jewish name?" I asked.

Nobody answered; Patrick just kept looking at Betty.

Alfredo pushed his head around the door:

"Are you ready yet?"

"Come in," I said.

He stood there defiantly looking at them:

"Well?"

"You'll have to fuck off somewhere else," I said, "Patrick doesn't like Jews."

He laughed so much I thought he was putting it on.

"I didn't say that," said Patrick, "as far as I'm concerned you can move in tomorrow."

"Thursday," said Alfredo, "Thursday will be better for me," he shook Betty by the hand. "Is it a deal?"

He looked at us; it was okay by me and the whole situation amused me because I don't think Patrick wanted him to stay - he just didn't have the guts to say so.

"See you Thursday." said Alfredo and left.

Betty sat back down again with a look of bewilderment on her face and Patrick stood up: "I don't know about you two but it's time for a Martini. Do you want one?"

"Yes," I said.

"He didn't even say what time on Thursday," said Betty.

He didn't have to bother because on Thursday, when I got up at midday, he was already in his room. I didn't know where Betty was but Alfredo was holding a dustpan and brush and sweeping around the window ledge when I looked in: "This place is filthy," he said.

"How did you get in?" I asked.

"Through the window!" and he said that as if I had asked a stupid question.

His belongings were piled up in the corner and his old car was parked outside in the drive.

"You won't be able to leave the car there," I said, "Betty will be wanting access the garage at the back."

"I'd already figured that one out," was all he had to say, and he carried on dusting.

I left him to his own devices so I could try and get on with my day. My day usually started with having breakfast: a cup of coffee, black, and a cigarette; I couldn't smoke in the kitchen so I would stand by the back door and look at the back yard.

Alfredo came out as I was taking my last drag of the fag and wanted to know which day the garbage went out:

"It went out this morning," I said.

"God damn," he said, softly, punching his fist lightly into the air as he had done the first time I saw him that evening on Highland.

"What do you want to know for?"

"I have something to put in to the garbage."

"You mean you brought rubbish with you?"

"Yeh: the bags and packing and some papers I have."

"Put them into the bin. It'll go next week."

This seemed to fox him. He said he didn't want his waste being in the bin for the whole week:

"You never know who might get at it," he said.

Then he noticed that I had been smoking:

"That'll kill you!" he said.

That was it for the moment, with Alfredo, as I had to go to work.

2

The house was very lively when I came home at around nine-thirty in the evening. Patrick had lit the big fire and filled it with logs. It was blazing invitingly in the fireplace and reminding me of home. The place smelt wonderful and he had been barbequing on the front porch: sausages, chicken and pork chops. I was hoping some was for me as I was broke and had only eaten a slice of pizza from the Pizza Factory on Sunset on the way home.

"Did you eat dinner?" asked Patrick.

I shrugged:

"Could you eat something?"

"Yes," I said.

With that he went into the kitchen to get me something. I could hear the rattling of pots and pans and he came back with a plate full of food.

"Here we are," he said, like a parent welcoming a son home from school.

As he put the food onto the table Alfredo came out of his door.

"How's that?" Patrick said "You do like pork chops and chicken and sausage don't you?"

"Yes," I said.

"It's pork sausage," he said, "Alfredo! Do you want some of this?

"No thanks," said Alfredo.

He nodded to me and then jumped back into his room saying:

"Look what I have here!"

He hopped back out with a five stringed banjo:

"How about that?"

He stood back with a huge grin on his face. He had spoken to me about the banjo on our walks together, and said I could play it any time I wanted. It looked fine sitting there but I had to eat what Patrick had given me first.

Patrick looked disdainfully at the banjo as if it was something far beneath him.

"When are the minstrels coming?" he said.

Alfredo went back into his room ignoring Patrick's crass remark.

"I'll be giving this to the dog next-door," shouted Patrick, "are you sure?"

"Give it to the dog," Alfredo called from his room.

As I ate my meal Patrick was finding logs for the fire; now and again he would go out to tend to his barbeque but I could see he was doing this to try and get a look at Alfredo through his window; then he would come back and whisper something to Betty; Betty would take his information then go out and look for herself then they would both come back and giggle. I couldn't hear what they were saying as the fireplace was at the other end of the large room.

The banjo was easy to tune and I played a few scales on it.

"Play one of your Irish songs," said Betty.

"My name is McNamara I'm the leader of the band," sang Patrick.

"I don't think that's an Irish song," she said.

It was about as Irish as he was! All he had, like the song, was an Irish name: Patrick Conroy.

I started to strum on the banjo and then went into "The Banks of the Roses" which is a traditional Irish song. I just strummed and sang and Patrick pulled Betty up by the hand to dance and we had the atmosphere of being back home; Alfredo came out of his room and started clapping his hands in rhythm with the beat and I was stamping my foot, strumming the strings and belting out the lyrics for our hooley.

"Having a bit of a hooley are we now?" shouted Alfredo.

I nodded my head and carried on singing.

"What's a hooley?" shouted Betty.

"A party," shouted Alfredo, as he carried on clapping.

Then he picked up a couple of spoons from the table and started to play them bones style; as he played bits of food came off the end.

I finished the song and they gave me a huge round of applause and Patrick poured a beer for me.

"Thanks," I said.

I took a gigantic swig and then went straight into another favourite song of mine "Whiskey in the Jar."

Whilst I was singing this I noticed Patrick, as he danced with Betty, do something to her; I don't know what it was, it might have been a little pinch or a nudge, I'm not sure, but her reaction was kind of conspiratorial as if they had something going between them and she stealthily stopped him doing whatever it was I almost missed.

I had lived with them in the house for three months and this was the first time I had noticed any sign of a relationship. Patrick had moved in maybe two weeks before I did, just after the New Year a week or two before I first met Alfredo. So the four of us were starting out on any future prospective relationships and we knew very little about each other. Frighteningly little as Betty never asked for references preferring to trust to instinct. I never told her that the first time I met Alfredo he mentioned being thrown out of his last place.

Whilst I was singing the next song, Alfredo went back into his room and as soon as I finished he came back out with loads of paper, plastic bags and pieces of cardboard and dumped them onto the fire:

"There we are," he said, "that'll make a good blaze."

It didn't! It put the fire out and I didn't sing any more that night.

3

I thought the night when I came back and found the house warm and busy with Patrick doing all the cooking was in aid of Alfredo moving in and that they had invited him for dinner. But they hadn't. Before I came in Betty and Patrick had sat down and ate their meals by themselves. They had left Alfredo to his own devices. Patrick had made sure to buy and cook pork and made a special effort to light the fire. It was as if he was trying to sell Alfredo the idea that we were some kind of family unit and to beware of disturbing it.

He had cooked before for me when I had arrived home late from work but had spoiled it the following day by telling me how much it had cost him and asking me for a certain amount of money. I told him to fuck off and told him to shove the food up his arse if he was expecting me to pay for anything; he had invited me to eat, which is why I knew he wouldn't ask me for any money for that night; but I did wonder if he asked Betty. The idea of him making sure to cook pork on Alfredo's first evening was lost on me at the time and I only thought about it later. Maybe he was telling Alfredo that pork gets cooked in this house whether you are Jewish or not. It turned out that Alfredo was a vegetarian.

I had to go to work a little earlier the following day so I was up and out of bed at around nine-thirty. My day usually started with a very important visit to the bathroom but the bathroom door was shut. Being shut meant it was occupied, as there was no lock on any of the doors. I had a full bladder so went up to use Patrick and Betty's lavatory, which was upstairs. There was nobody up there and I thought back to the night before and looked where he or she might be creeping during the night – from his room to hers, from her room to his?

Patrick was in the kitchen, when I got there, looking for his newspapers.

"You got my LA Times?" He said "I want to see the box scores."

The baseball season had started and he said he was a keen fan of the New York Yankees. It gave him something to talk about when he was in a bar. He'd say to the barman:

"Who do you like?"

This would amuse me.

"Who do you like?" He'd say, and he'd call both the barman and the barmaid bartenders.

He knew where his 'LA Times' was; it was in the bathroom with Alfredo.

"He's been in there forty-five minutes" he said.

"Where's Betty?"

"Nothing to do with Betty" he said.

Betty was in the back garden fiddling about with the weeds and the flowers. She had a habit of retreating to the garden if ever she thought there might be some kind of confrontation; now and then we could hear her go into the cellar, which she called the cantina. I don't know why she called it that but as the house had been in the family since it had been built, maybe seventy five years earlier in nineteen twenty, I figured it was a kind of family nick name, some place where she had played as a child. The cantina had two entrances: the one directly below us was where she kept her gardening tools and the other entrance, which was under my bedroom, was used for junk. There were two old air conditioning units in there and a few cardboard boxes.

The place where she kept her gardening tools was very interesting: it looked as if it had been kept by a handyman as all the old nails were in special marked tins; there were various kinds of drills, hammers, saws, reamers and other pieces of carpentry equipment; lots of them in tiny cardboard nail boxes and there were lots of rulers and spirit levels too. It was the kind of place where it was good to stand and drink a cup of tea. I always loved the idea of a workman taking a tea break and sitting there sipping tea as he contemplated his next move; it struck me that it might be the only attraction in getting a job. The place had a great smell: a smell of tools, linseed oil and the smell of age.

I heard the bathroom door open and Alfredo came into the kitchen, with his usual big grin and the newspapers, all messed up, under his arm. He put them onto the butcher's block, which was in the centre of the room, and Patrick picked them up and took them to the breakfast table to read. He made a big fuss about them being ruffled. He didn't say anything just put them onto the table and started to spread them out making as much noise as possible as he flattened and ironed them with his hand. I half expected him to get the iron out and press them but he didn't. Alfredo just ignored him. He took oatmeal from his part of the cupboard and added loads of it to a pan. Then he sprinkled various herbs, raisins, dried bananas, dried sliced apple, cinnamon and other things, which I didn't recognise, into the mix. He opened the fridge and Patrick's water filter bottle was on the top shelf.

"What's this?"

"I put water in that from the faucet" said Patrick "and it filters through like pure water."

"What's the matter with the water in the tap?"

"Nothing" said Patrick, "but this is purer!"

"That's grand" said Alfredo as he removed the bottle top and poured a sizeable quantity of water over his oatmeal.

Patrick's face was a picture but I didn't wait, as I needed to take a shower. When I came back, Alfredo was on the way to his room with a large saucepan of porridge, he didn't believe in using plates, and I didn't see him again till I finished work.

4

I could never figure out what he was doing in his room. Sometimes I would think he was asleep when he would be at the desk writing. He would literally crawl out of bed and start to write. His visits to the bathroom were for over an hour each and sometimes even more. Then he would make the big breakfast of oatmeal and loads of cinnamon and the like and get back on with his work. At around four in the afternoon he would disappear to Runyan Canyon Park where he would hike for hours: Dog Shit Canyon, he called it.

In the evening he would find a super market to stock up with food, ice cream and large jars of apple sauce. I don't know how much ice cream he consumed each week but he thought nothing of sitting in front of his television set with a huge half a gallon tub and eating the lot in one sitting. Sometimes he would come out and talk to me in the kitchen whilst I was making my nightcap. He would stand and talk before disappearing into the garden where I would see him looking at the stars.

On top of the garage at the bottom of the garden was a guest house. Leading up to this there was a small wooden staircase with a flat surface, at the top, which formed a deck where Patrick sun bathed. Alfredo liked to stand on the flat surface and look at the stars. On a cloudy night he was troubled. If he had been eating a lot of ice cream his stay in the back garden would be cut short as he rushed to the bathroom to defecate, as he called it;

"I need to defecate I need to defecate," he would whisper as he ran as fast as he could to the house trying to keep his legs close together and the cheeks of his arse tight.

One night I joined him on the rostrum. I had returned from a night in Molly Malone's bar on Fairfax and I could see Alfredo as I ambled up the drive. He was staring towards the heavens on a very clear beautiful night. I went to the kitchen and took a glass of Patrick's vodka and joined him.

"What's going on?" I said "what's happening?"

He didn't say anything just kept looking at the celestial sky. Then he turned and said "I just heard six shots."

He didn't drink so I didn't offer him any. I was never sure if he had gone through a bout of alcoholism sometime in his life, as he seemed frightened of alcohol.

"Look up" he said "look up to the stars and what do you see?"

"What is the stars" I laughed quoting O'Casey.

"Not that" he said "just look."

I took a drink of my vodka and took another look.

"James Joyce had to look at those same stars" he said. "I've been to the planetarium to ask them to put the stars the same way as they were on June sixteenth nineteen-o-four."

"Did they do it?"

"Yes" he said "it was amazing!"

"You must have seen them as they looked over America" I said.

He thought for a moment:

"You're right!"

"Where were the shots from?"

He looked towards the end of the garden and vaguely pointed: "Over there," he said.

He didn't seem particularly bothered. There was no noise from back there; no police activity or people shouting.

After a pause he said: "Bloomsday is next week. You got anything planned for next Friday?"

"No."

"I want to go to an Irish theatre group at Fountain and Fairfax. They're doing some of Ulysses. Do you want to come?"

"Yes" I said.

I knew that people walked around Dublin on each June sixteenth to celebrate Bloomsday and visit all the bars that were mentioned in Ulysses, which took part on that famous day but as with Saint Patrick, it didn't seem important to me when I lived there but in Los Angeles it was different.

"There'll be helicopters here soon" but he was wrong.

5

Alfredo didn't like the production at the Bloomsday celebration: I could see that. I liked it as they performed pieces of Ulysses that I knew: one was an excerpt from the Nighttown episode, which made me laugh. I looked towards Alfredo, as I laughed, and his face seemed to be in pain. When one of the girls was doing a monologue a newspaper critic shouted out:

"Speak up Gertie, I can't hear you!"

I could tell he was a critic as he was sitting with a clipboard on his lap and when he spoke Alfredo gave me strange look. He thought it interesting that we could see up the girl's frock as she sat doing her monologue and he whispered to me: "Are we supposed to be seeing next week's laundry?"

I laughed!

The street lights were out when we left the theatre. Some kind of major electrical outage as it also affected the traffic lights at the junction of Fairfax and Fountain Avenues so we couldn't even see the hands in front of our faces. Not that we had our hands in front of our faces but if we did we wouldn't be able to see them. We had to risk life and limb to cross the street.

Alfredo took it as a kind of omen.

"What do you see?"

"What?" I replied.

"The stars! Look up."

We both looked up and it was a clear night. There were a few cars around and they were too busy trying to cross the Fairfax-Fountain junction to worry about two pedestrians, but Alfredo didn't take his eyes away from the stars as he crossed Fountain to the north side.

"Look, at that" he said, and he stopped walking. He had spotted something in the sky. Something that affected him emotionally which was in his voice as he almost recited:

"The lights in Los Angeles went out on Bloomsday!"

We looked up the hill towards Sunset and everything was black. Usually, when traffic lights fail in Los Angeles, the red light flashes and the rules of the road change to that of a four-way-stop. I mentioned this to Alfredo:

"That is one of the most telling things about the Americans" he said "or maybe just the Angelinos. In an emergency they click into 'emergency mode' – plan 'B' - but then, on the other hand, it shows me that they are fucking brainwashed."

They didn't do that this night though. Everything was in darkness. I couldn't really see him, as we walked, so his deep Dublin accented voice seemed to come to me through the darkness.

I had only been in Los Angeles, indeed America, for six months so everything was still new to me but with the eyes of a novice I could see things that the natives probably didn't see and which I would cease to notice eventually.

"They only use one word for everything "he said. "Did you not notice that gobshite on the door at the theatre?"

I had asked the fella on the door, at the theatre, if there was an interval and the fella didn't understand me. He was supposed to be an Irish-American but was probably standing as close to Ireland as he had ever been so his word for interval was intermission.

"Oh! Do you mean intermission?" he had said.

This would happen on many occasions as I got to know the language of America realising, eventually, that it was a language made up of words and phrases from the rest of the world and the American Indian languages. Because the majority of the people who used English were American their use of it would influence the rest of the English speaking world and in time would wipe out many languages leaving just one. The one left will be the American English Language with its one word for everything lowest common denominator limited vocabulary language. These thoughts went through my head more often than I wanted them to after Alfredo had pointed them out to me but not on this night; the night of the Bloomsday blackout. My vocabulary was limited enough without having it limited even more.

Alfredo mentioned the Indians as we traced our way along Fountain Avenue in search for his old car.

"This is what it was like for the Indians," he said "This is how dark it was for them. You never see an Indian here and this is their country. The white man came along and fucked them off to oblivion but you know" and he stopped walking again, "can you blame them for not wanting to fight at night? The poor bastards! The poor fuckers kicked out of their land to make way for the settlers. You should read about the trail of tears or, to translate it from the Cherokee, 'the trail where they cried."

"Do you speak Cherokee?"

"Don't be a gobshite."

"I'll try and read something about it" I said.

He laughed at this: "You'll need to read a lot of books by the time I'm finished with you."

There seemed to be a complete lack of traffic along Fountain Avenue, so our way wasn't even lit by the headlights of cars. The neighbourhood was not the safest of places to be at that time of night and the thought of being stuck up by somebody with a gun crossed my mind a few times. The lack of cars also made it very quiet, which wasn't natural for that part of town.

Alfredo's car seemed to be parked further away than I had imagined and I didn't know where we were.

"Do you know where we are?" I asked "Do you know where we're going?"

"Follow me" he said striding forward like the wagon train scout he thought he was.

As he walked ahead we could see in the near distance the glow of a cigarette butt. He started to walk real fast when he saw it, leaving me behind, and when he got closer we could see it was a girl. He slowed down and waited for me and she said "Good night for a party, boys?"

Alfredo gave her a strange look then turned to me and said "Nighttown!"

He giggled as we walked on and said "Did you see the instinct of the survivor? I put space between us. I surrounded the enemy."

Him and his imagination!

I couldn't understand why there was so little traffic and when we turned into Ogden Avenue it got even creepier; all the houses with their lights out and a few people standing in the front gardens. There were more trees in Ogden, which made it a lot darker, and some of the people were leaning on the trees or sitting on the tree stumps. They were mumbling to each other, which was strange: normally when Angelinos want to talk they talk out loud and don't care what time of day or night it is. They laugh out loud, shout and scream, if they feel like it, no matter who is trying to sleep or get some peace. This time it was weird. It was as if some bomb had exploded and we were walking through the aftermath of a holocaust. We walked passed people smoking dope, we could smell it, looking at us as if they were in a dream and we were reality stopping by. But we didn't stop by we looked and made our way to the car which Alfredo seemed to know the whereabouts of all the time. When we had almost reached Sunset Boulevard we got to the car; clipped to the screen was a parking ticket.

"Fucking place," Alfredo said as he ripped it from under the wiper, "getting a parking ticket at ten-o-clock at night!"

I looked around at the darkened street "Look over there" he said.

"What?"

"Over there – look at that tree."

There was a very strange shaped tree on the other side of the street.

"I think it's a jacaranda tree" he said "but look at the shape. It's two jays; James Joyce!"

I thought it looked like two esses but he saw two jays.

Three people from the street were standing around it. They had put a couple of candles on the horizontal bits which they frequently used to light whatever it was they were smoking. It seemed to light the tree up.

"If that's not an omen I don't know what is. We are in a street named after a poet. "

"Who?" I said.

"Ogden Nash."

"How do you know this wasn't here before Ogden Nash?" I said.

"I don't!" he said "but what you don't know doesn't mean shite. We are in a street named after a poet, on the night of the Bloomsday blackout and the tree we are looking at is shaped like James Joyce's initials."

"Or Sarah Siddons" I said.

"Who?"

"Sarah Siddons: the English actress."

"What a load of shite – I'm inspired and you talk of an English actress."

He didn't say anything he just looked at the tree as if it was the second coming; the people around it looked over at us. One was a woman of around fifty five who was sitting on the kerb; she had black heavily made up eyes, with the mascara running down her face and long black hair and when Alfredo opened his window she looked over at him and said "Farinelli!" When she said this she clenched her open fist as if she was castrating Alfredo.

He laughed as he started the motor.

"What was that about?"

"There's a movie playing in West LA called Farinelli about a castrato."

"The trail of tears?"

"Yes" he laughed "it would certainly make your eyes water."

He got the parking ticket and kissed it then he flung it into the back.

"But I'm inspired" he said "I'm inspired."

"How come you know so much about Indians?" I asked.

'You should know. The Indians are like the Irish. Like the Irish before Christianity hit Ireland; in any case I'm a John Ford fan."

6

Alfredo's play, the one that was half written and which the movie star was interested in, was about James Joyce and his wife Nora. It was set on the last night Joyce spent on this earth and retraced various aspects of his life. Alfredo's plan was to finish writing the play and get it put on in Los Angeles as a showpiece. He arranged lots of meetings with people at small Equity waiver theatre companies. One day he found one that was interested in doing a rehearsed reading of the finished script. Of course he had to finish it.

"Will you play Joyce?"

"Me?" I said "I'm too young. Maybe in another twenty years."

"Ah don't be worrying about that" he said "you have the voice."

"I don't know" – and I didn't.

"I've talked to them and they want George Segal or John Saxon to do it. I want an Irish voice."

"At least George Segal is Jewish. It might work."

"Joyce wasn't Jewish" he said. "Bloom was!"

"Why would they want George Segal or John Saxon?"

"It's Hollywood."

He never gave up and asked me to play Joyce periodically over the next few months. Things would get quiet at night and he would join me and say:

"You know you'd be very good. I want your voice."

But it wasn't to be. I wasn't an actor.

****

7

My mother called me one morning from Dublin: as far as she was concerned she was calling her big son in Los Angeles for an afternoon chat. Unfortunately she didn't realise that it was five-o-clock in the morning where I lived and woke me from a sound sleep. It happened a few times and as it didn't sink in no matter how many times I told her I got into the habit of turning my phone off before getting into bed – click – then I knew I would get some sleep. It was the best thing I ever did because when Alfredo didn't pay his rent that first month Betty called me at seven-o-clock one morning. When she found out that she would be going straight to my voice mail she called me every morning at seven-o-clock. I think she was using it as some kind of therapy. She would go on and on about Alfredo and not just about the rent: Could you tell him this? Could you tell him that? Can you get him to take his underwear out of the bathroom? Can you stop him taking the electric fan into the bathroom and leaving it on before he takes a bath? Can you tell him to wait till he gets into the bathroom before running the water? If he can't pay the rent he should sell that expensive computer!

Alfredo had the terrible habit of going into the bathroom to run the bath water and then he would go back into his room and get on with his writing. The inspiration from the stars in the heavens would hit him and an hour or so later one of us would go into the bathroom to see the cold water disappearing down the overflow. It was a great inconvenience to all of us but I'm not sure if it needed daily phone calls to me: maybe just one to him?

When Alfredo did his laundry he would take his clothes out to the garden and dump them over the clothesline. He didn't use his clothes pegs, or pins as the Americans called them, to spread the items out and sometimes, if you saw them at night, they looked like ghostly figures standing in the garden. He left them draped over the clothesline for days at a time on many occasions. Sometimes his clothes were on the line for weeks: Can you tell Alfredo to take his laundry in as I have visitors tomorrow!

I listened to every phone message intently but never passed one message on.

He was a handful to live with but I liked him.

For some reason he frightened Betty and I could see Patrick didn't approve of him. But Patrick never said a word. He would just sit there and let the world go into one ear and out the other unless it was sports.

The fact that Alfredo was behind in his rent was nothing to do with me. I had introduced him to the household but Betty seemed to think that I was his keeper and responsible for him because of that or maybe because we were both Irish.

She called her Congressman every day. At six-o-clock in the morning she would use a free number and complain about whatever was on her mind. Her telephone was in the main room of the house and she spoke so loudly that she woke Alfredo nearly every morning. Then she would go into the kitchen, dry the dishes and put them into the cupboard. The noise she made putting the dishes into the cupboard would wake me up as I slept close to the wall on the other side of it. My only solution was to make sure all dishes were dried and put away before going to bed. After this she would go into the garden and call me on the telephone and rant about Alfredo. She would speak into the phone with her soap opera out of work actress voice technique and complain to my voice mail as if she was reading from a list she had made the day before of the happenings of the monster in the front room; the monster that would have been laying in its slumber if Betty had not disturbed it.

She had a problem with men and the fact that this particular man had a bit of a problem with women did something to her. I was never sure of her history. I know she had a daughter somewhere but she never mentioned the father of her children. I didn't get to find out if she was a single parent, divorced, widowed or anything; not that it was any of my business; I knew that she had a boyfriend, around her age, who was some kind of publisher. He was called Harold and he would take her anywhere she wanted to go but she treated him like a piece of shit.

One day he was up at the guest house:

"What are you doing up there, Harold?" she shouted.

When he called for her he would bring with him a bag of goodies: boxes of chocolates, magazines and anything else, which he thought might take her fancy.

"I'm just putting your snack bag up here" he called back.

That's what he called the weekly presents.

But there was no 'oh thank you for the gifts' but "Well, you're not allowed up there" she screamed "I've just done the floor. Get it down and put it into the house."

He did as he was told. When he came into the kitchen he said "We're going to see Doctor Zhivago for the thirtieth time."

"Thirtieth?" I said

"Yes. I've seen it every year since its release and this is the thirtieth anniversary."

"Does Betty like it?"

He didn't answer. Maybe she didn't and that was how he got his own back!

He put the bag into the large fridge at the back and put the magazines onto the butcher's block. Then he picked up Betty's bags, as she was staying over at his place for the weekend, and he walked out the back door with them.

"Where are you you going with my bags?" she called after him.

"You said . . . ."

"Put them in the car, Harold." she interrupted.

He did an about turn like an unquestioning old infantryman and took the bags to his car. When he had done that he came back in to me in the kitchen and said "Have a good one" then he left with Betty following him.

As if he had been listening to this from around the doorway Alfredo came into the kitchen "She may treat one Jew like a piece of shit but not this one!" he said.

"He says he is. But why would a Jew flee Germany and go to Cuba *after* the war?"

"I don't know" I said "maybe he's the son of a Nazi?"

"He said he won't go back to Germany because they gasses his people; maybe it's the other way around?"

Then he opened the big fridge and saw the goody bag.

"Oh?" he said in a mock shock kind of way "what are these so withered and so wild in their attire? They must be for us?"

He turned around and smiled at me as he took lots of chocolate bars.

"Want some?" he said.

"For fuck sake Alfredo" I said "get a brain."

He went into his room murmuring something about the son of a Nazi.

8

Patrick spent many weekends away. His family lived in Florida and had friends in New York and Wyoming. He wasn't in the habit of telling us where he was at any particular time and neither did Betty. I just happened to be sitting in the kitchen on the Saturday evening that Harold put the goodies into the fridge but if I had been out I wouldn't have known if Betty was spending the evening under the roof or not, and, by the same token, they never knew about me. The only person who had a clue about my whereabouts was Alfredo. It would be quite possible for one of us to go missing and not be missed at all for days.

One day, Patrick asked me to photograph the inside of the house. He wanted photographs of his bedroom, the bathroom, which he shared with Betty, and the main living room. He had borrowed Betty's camera but couldn't figure out how to use it. It seemed simple enough to me: load the film, turn it on and point it. It had automatic flash so I couldn't see what could go wrong.

"What about the garden?"

"No" he said "it looks too nice."

It did; it looked like paradise.

When I had taken the pictures I unloaded the film and gave it to him for processing.

A couple of days later he showed me the pictures and I was very pleased with the results. So was Patrick but for a different reason. I didn't know much about early twentieth century furniture and decorative arts but I could see the house was filled with good examples of it; there was a mini grand piano in the living room, which was dominated by silver-framed pictures and a *Dirk Van Erp* lamp, which I learned later was worth a fortune; a full fireplace with mantlepiece and various sizes and shapes of candlesticks from the nineteen twenties; a very large fitted glass fronted bookcase, was at the back of the room, full of old books, pieces of porcelain, old collectible kitchen utensils and various pieces of flatware; a large oak dining room table was in front of the bookcase, which had six or seven dining room chairs around it, and there were lots of tasteful pieces of bric-a-brac filling any unnecessary holes or spaces throughout the large room.

Every time I brought a girl home I could measure their tastes by what they appreciated about the house and they, in turn, taught me what to look for in the world of furniture and decorative arts. Most of the intelligent arty types would point out the craftsmanship of the front door and the door to Alfredo's room, which was almost next to it. When Alfredo's door was mentioned I would warn them that it may be a fine example of craftsmanship but they didn't know what it concealed and what lurked behind it. If Alfredo was in and heard me he would open the door quickly and frighten the girl.

He didn't look violent or weird but seemed to frighten women and homosexuals: maybe it was the way he didn't do anything to his eyebrows or his wild white hair. It could have been the way he looked at people or the way he didn't. He wasn't a bully but he frightened the weak.

A curious thing about Alfredo's room was that there were two doors. One from the living room and one from the back of his room which lead directly to the hall which led to my room, passing the over used bathroom on its way. Then the hall bent left and back onto the living room again.

The photographs I took for Patrick made the house look quite classy and when Betty saw them she was delighted.

"These are perfect" said Patrick "they show the squalor I have to live in."

The poor ignorant eejit thought he was an expert on antiques but he knew nothing without a label.

9

It took me a few weeks to figure it out. He was going through a divorce so needed to show that he lived in the poorest of conditions. The fact that he didn't appreciate the treasures just showed how ignorant he was to the finer things in life. I didn't necessarily know too much about collectable twentieth century furniture and decorative arts or the 'Arts and Crafts' movement myself, but I could see that it had a certain amount of quality and interest.

There was a documentary on the television one night about Woody

Guthrie and it featured his song 'This Land is Our Land,' which he wrote in response to 'God Bless America;' Patrick had never heard of either the song or Woody Guthrie.

I was having breakfast with him in Duke's Coffee Shop on Sunset Boulevard, one day, and there was a large photograph of Jim Morrison on the wall. I asked him if he knew who it was. He shrugged his shoulders and said "John Lennon?"

Everybody doesn't have to know who Jim Morrison was or what John Lennon looked like but when somebody gives you that type of answer it lets you know with whom you might be dealing.

One of his annoying pastimes was to throw a tennis ball, baseball style, at the garage door. Most of the times it came back to him and he would pitch again.

Up his leg would come and 'wush' the ball would be hitting the door. He might have been a good pitcher but the speed of the ball was impeded, as it wasn't a proper baseball.

I asked him why baseball pitchers lifted their leg and he said they had to. Then he explained why they had to and it sounded as clear as mud.

The pitching of the ball would annoy the dog next door as he thought the ball was being thrown for him but he couldn't get it as he couldn't get through the fence. The thump thump thumping of the ball on the door would annoy everybody else and he had the other annoying habit of pretending to be deaf when he was being shouted at to stop. On top of that the dog would be barking. So there was the thumping, the shouting for him to stop and the dog barking, him shouting 'aye' which added up to a good impression of Bedlam!

Once in a while I would grab a piece of wood and use it as a bat. I had played a lot of cricket so a tennis ball coming at me at the height he was throwing the pitches was no problem and I could knock some of his pitches over the roof. The whole process frustrated the dog even more. Patrick would find this hilarious. I never played for any length of time: just a few knocks on my way out to work. Alfredo saw me playing a couple of times and thought I was quite good but I wasn't. It was a tennis ball coming at me waist high and that was easy.

"I'll have a go one of the days" Alfredo shouted .

He didn't look like an athlete, even though he walked like a boxer, always with a spring in his step, but physical things were beyond him: he didn't seem to have any coordination. His exercise was limited to *Dog Shit Canyon* or Griffith Park and most of the time he would take the dog from next door with him. The dog would look forward to it and it would even take its attention away from the tennis ball pitching if Alfredo made an appearance at the front door in his shorts and hiking boots carrying his stick. Round his waist he would have his wallet which he wouldn't go anywhere without it as it contained his complete works on a floppy disc from his computer. One day he left it in his car, by mistake, while he went off for the hike. It wasn't until he got a mile away from the car that he realized he had left it. So he went back and it was gone. Somebody had taken it. He leaned on his stick and stood there in despair when the dog brought the bag to him. His money had been taken but the thief had discarded the wallet with the floppy discs.

I asked him how much money was missing.

"All I had" he said, "thirty-five cents."

Patrick on the other hand was a mystery. He said he came from Boston and went to a Latin school but if I asked him to translate any simple Latin he hadn't a clue. He was also a fan of the New York Yankees and you don't get many Yankee fans in Boston which is the home of the Red Sox.

****

10

Whenever I called my mother in Dublin, before going to work, she would call me straight back as I could never afford a big phone bill. I could hear the Angelus Bell ringing on her television. She said she would always think of me when the bell rang as I was in Angeles: "The Lost Angelus" she would say.

It was somehow comforting to hear the sounds of home as I was off in a far off land pursuing a dream. I never knew what the dream was but I was sure it would come to me one day. Was I going to write the great screenplay, discover myself as an actor or raise money from the rich and make an independent film? Who knew? I certainly didn't. The fact that I had to work took some of the adventure out of the adventure. My mother wanted me to get married and settle down. This wasn't out of the question but I wanted to see what life was going to offer me first. She thought I was gallivanting in Hollywood with all the stars because I told her I had seen Dennis Franz, who was one of the stars from NYPD Blue, one day. She had rarely watched that particular TV show but after I told her of my meeting she never missed an episode and even referred to him as my friend. She would say "Your friend was very good tonight! He has to watch his temper."

I didn't have the heart to argue with her and tell her I had only met him in a lift at a multi-storey car park. In fact the word met is hardly the right one, as we didn't even speak.

When I saw another actor from NYPD Blue at a filling station with Patrick one day I didn't mention it to my mother. She would be having visions of me out with my two pals cruising the Sunset Strip.

Sometimes she would make me late, as she liked to talk to me and hear about my life with the stars. One day I came out, after talking to her, and Patrick was throwing the tennis ball at the garage door. But this time the fella with the bat was Alfredo. He was hopeless. Betty was watching too and throwing the ball back to Patrick as it bounced off the garage door behind Alfredo, as it bounced off Alfredo's shoulder, his head and even knocking his sunglasses off at one point. They were trying to humiliate him. "Come out of the way," I said to Alfredo "I'll have a go."

The poor dog next door was in a terrible state. It didn't know if it was going for a walk with Alfredo or whether to run up and down after the ball. It decided to get really nasty with Patrick, which was a natural thing for anybody to do. Each time the dog barked and growled at him Patrick would taunt it again making it bark and growl even louder. The woman from next door came out to see who was annoying her dog and Alfredo ran round to pacify the poor animal as soon as he let go of the bat. As soon as the dog saw Alfredo coming it ran to him and he fussed it and loved it with such care as it wagged its tail and licked Alfredo's face.

I had grabbed the made up feeble looking excuse for a bat from Alfredo and Patrick took it as a challenge. He started to wind up like a Yankee pitcher facing the Red Sox.

I stood there with the bat in position to hit the ball out of Maltman Avenue and into Sunset Boulevard which was a couple of hundred yards away. No chance really but I was shaping up to do it nonetheless "Now you're for it limey" he shouted.

"I'm not a fucking limey!" I said.

"Oh, listen to him" he said, and he started to bring his leg up and then put it back down. Then he hit the ball in the palm of his other hand and stared at me with a strange look on his face that he probably thought was a threat.

As Patrick let the ball fly I dropped the bat. He had aimed at my knees and I could, conceivably have hit it good and proper, but I decided to catch it and I threw it straight back at him. His reflexes were quicker than Alfredo's so he ducked and the ball went into the street.

He and Betty took the whole incident as some kind of joke but I didn't think it was funny. They were humiliating that poor old man because he was different from them. He was probably ten years younger than they were but Patrick was the sporty type with his tracksuits and trainers on all the time, except when he went for an audition when he would wear the blue suit. He looked like an executive in the suit.

11

On July fourth the Americans went away. Patrick went to stay with one of his sons and Betty went to stay with her daughter in Las Vegas. I don't know how she got to Las Vegas, or whether she played in the casinos when she got there; I was never sure if she had tackled Alfredo about his lack of rent but it didn't make any difference where she spent the night as she called me every morning and gave me the same litany of complaints about Alfredo. She had three minutes to get everything off her chest because that was the maximum amount of time the telephone company would allow for an individual message; and it was a good job; maybe she would have gone on for hours without that restriction.

July the fourth was also Alfredo's third month without paying rent. He had given Betty a certain amount of money in April, when he moved in, and that was it; but it didn't matter how many months he was behind with his rent Betty was only getting three minutes of airtime on my answer phone. The other thing she would complain about was his addiction to ice cream.

"He spends a fortune on ice cream" she would say "and he should be paying me rent."

One of her favourite expressions was 'It's not the cheap stuff he buys!'

Sometimes she would just talk about his expensive computer.

This July the fourth was my first July the fourth in America and when I went into the street people wished me a happy fourth. A very strange thing to hear with the foreign ear but I noticed that the Latinos didn't say it. They were their usual polite selves without ever mentioning it.

Alfredo came into the kitchen when I was making my morning coffee and sat down at the table next to me. He had a knowing look on his face which turned to a smile.

"Guess who's got a job?" he said.

"A killing?"

"Not yet" he replied.

He knew a film producer. The producer liked the fact that he was Irish-Jewish; had a background of folk music, rock music, Haight-Ashbury and a San Francisco nineteen sixties hippy attitude. So he had arranged a rendezvous with an American writer with whom he thought Alfredo would be able to get on with both personally and professionally. He was wrong, of course. I was the only person who Alfredo ever got on with. I was the only person who could tell him to fuck off and he knew I wouldn't stand any of his nonsense. He liked the fact that I would encourage him to commit suicide if he ever threatened it; and threaten it he did all the time. Sometimes I could see he was desperate and I would listen to his troubles for hours but it would bring a smile to his face when I would answer his question of: 'What do you think I should do?' with 'There's no hope! You better kill yourself.'

I was never sure if I was saying the right thing, of course, and was never sure of the state of his mental health. I knew he was taking something called ZOLOFT on prescription. Whoever was paying for the prescription or where it was coming from I didn't know. It could be coming from his family in Ireland or his friends in Canada or San Francisco - or maybe even from somebody in Los Angeles; I never asked.

He had been to a meeting at the British Pub in Hollywood called The Cat and the Fiddle where the film producer wanted to introduce Alfredo to the American writer. The meeting was a disaster as Alfredo started off by trying to break the writer's balls. He told me that he was only joking but the writer didn't grasp any of the jokes. The producer and the writer ordered food and drinks but Alfredo refused anything apart from water of which he drank three pints. Every time they tried to eat anything they felt nervous when Alfredo watched their every move and munch with a stare and a sip. The writer left the meeting early leaving the film producer to look at Alfredo and wonder how he ever got the idea that he would be able to work with anybody.

A few days after the meeting, the producer called Alfredo and offered him a commission to write a first draft treatment for a feature film. The fee was to be seven hundred and fifty dollars. If the treatment was acceptable Alfredo would get over one hundred thousand dollars for a final draft screenplay.

"That's great" I said "he must like you after all!"

"Ah, he's a schlepper" he said and that was what we called the film producer from then on.

"We'll start work on it right away" he said.

"Hang on" I said "we'll? We'll? Where did the 'we' come from? And what about the James Joyce play? When are you going to finish that?"

"I'll get to that eventually" he said.

I could see the plans I had made for the day being kicked into touch. I had planned to sit out in the garden and get some sun.

"Got something to do?"

"No!" I said

"Okay! Tonight we start work."

12

That evening, as it was getting dark, I went to the supermarket on the corner of Sunset and Maltman to buy some beer. It was just down the street and on the way back I passed the house of a family of Mexicans having a birthday party. July the fourth seemed irrelevant to them. In their front yard they had placed loads of chairs in a line, then a space of about ten feet and then a table, which was full of all kinds of delicious looking and smelling food. Balloons were all over the place and the song on the record player was Speedy Gonzales.

Not the Pat Boone version as it was in Spanish. I didn't know there was a Spanish version as I thought the Pat Boone version was his usual white way of stereotyping the Mexicans. I didn't know he had been stealing musical ideas from them as he'd done from black singers in the nineteen fifties. It sounded good!

I hovered as I came up to the house, which I had seen on the way to the supermarket, in the hope that they might see me and invite me in. I was carrying a six-pack of Mexican beer so I could have contributed to the drinks tray but none of the people really saw me so I walked back on up the hill to where I had come from.

Just before I opened the door to go back to Alfredo I looked up and I could see rockets exploding and making beautiful patterns in the darkened Silverlake sky. I opened up a beer, sat on the front porch and witnessed my first July the fourth celebration, by myself, from the comfort of Betty's swing.

****

13

Alfredo had been given a piece of paper by the Schlepper. It contained about fifteen or twenty lines of type. The treatment he was to write concerned an American politician who faked his own death then came back under an assumed identity as a Country and Western Singer. I wasn't sure if it was supposed to be a comedy or a tragedy. I told Alfredo that an English politician named John Stonehouse had tried to fake his death in the nineteen seventies. He seemed to think this was a great piece of information and a couple of days later when I came in from work there were a couple of books on my bed: one was about American politics and the other contained a little bit about John Stonehouse; he had borrowed the books from the public library.

There was nobody in the house and he had gone out with the dog on his nightly hike. At least that's what I presumed he had done. I knocked on his door and went into his room; it was strangely quiet. There was a kind of ticking, as if he had a clock somewhere, and I could see his lap top computer on the desk below the place he slept, his telephone, with the very large dial, and the banjo in the corner. It seemed like a million years since the party on that first night but it was only three months. As I left the room one of the floorboards creaked.

He came back a few hours later and greeted me with the usual big smile. He would describe himself as a cheerful depressant; something the Americans would call an oxymoron. His plan was to write a screenplay as opposed to a treatment. He said it would knock them off their feet when they read it. He wanted me to look at the books and give him a few tips and then read his screenplay before he gave it to the Schlepper; I agreed. He told me he would grind me into the ground if I asked for any money and said he would believe the one hundred thousand dollars for the screenplay when he received it.

****

14

Riding on the bus was an experience to say the least and I would tell Alfredo about some of the characters I saw; he said I should make a diary.

About ten days or so after the July the fourth break Alfredo took a bus ride into Hollywood and back to show me what he meant. He said he got off where I got off when going up Highland Avenue, crossed over Hollywood Boulevard and took the next bus home.

I was about to go to work when he returned. I asked him if he saw anything interesting.

"Interesting' he said "I'll say."

"I was sitting on the bus next to two black dudes. I would say they were around thirty five and the description 'dude' sums up their appearances: one of them wore a khaki shirt and the other one wore a fleck jacket which had a saxophone broach on a lapel. I was sitting on a side seat, which faces the centre of the bus near the back, and they were in the long back seat. From what I could gather they were in the music business."

"You saw this today? Just now?"

"Yes – just now."

I sat down at the kitchen table and he stood in front of me as if about to perform.

"On the side seat next to me was a big black woman breastfeeding her little baby;" he said: "her two older children, a girl of seventeen and a boy of fourteen, were also with her and they were looking after the pushchair. The boy wore his baseball cap back-to-front and also wore tee shirt and jeans.

The black dudes were speaking very loudly:

"I dow wan dat bitch gettn no cred; she din write no song so she get no cred."

His impression of black dialogue was really funny and sounded authentic to me.

"He gave his pal a fierce look:

"You check it out man."

Alfredo looked at me:

"I don't know what he meant by that bit and they were very loud but the bus driver topped them over the public address system with:

'Next stop the world famous Hollywood and Vine."

He laughed when he said that and said it again:

"Next stop the world famous Hollywood and Vine. I was looking around for the dancers."

He did a little dance; then he sat at the table and pretended to be the driver moving his hands around an imaginary steering wheel.

"Fare must be paid" he said "and the driver looked at the woman next to where I was sitting. The daughter gave her mother a few bucks but the mother couldn't get out of her seat as she had one of her tits working – feeding the baby. So she gave the money to the young boy to take it to the driver. When he came back she said to him 'Where's the transfer?'

Then to her daughter 'Go get the transfer.'

The daughter sent the boy to the driver again and the momma carried on feeding the baby under her huge red tee shirt.

As the little lad made his way up the moving bus the two black dudes walked down the aisle to get off the bus "I ain't gonna pay that bitch no money...."

Their voices faded as they got off the bus so I didn't hear the end of that story."

He looked at me

"It's like a movie isn't it? Like Orson Welles with the sound fading in and out.

The son came back to his momma very subdued and sat beside her rubbing his head on her arm for reassurance: obviously no dice. Momma to the daughter:

'You keep sending him and I'm sending you! Now you go! You go get my transfers!'

The daughter shot out of her seat and went up to the driver. Then she came back equally subdued: 'Momma, she said."

I loved the way Alfredo did the little girl's voice:

'Momma,' she said. 'we ain't getting no transfers without no more money: that's what he said Momma.' She had a tear in her voice.

Momma saw red and it wasn't just her red tee shirt. She jumped out of her seat holding the baby with one arm. As she did so her tit came out of the child's mouth – I tell you I thought it was going to hit me - but she adjusted it in her stride and popped it back into the child's mouth. As she moved to the front of the bus her voice got louder the closer she got to the driver "You call them motherfucking powleece. I want my motherfucking transfer, y'asshole. You picked up the wrong person today you motherfucking asshole."

My stop was coming up so I left momma shouting at the driver and wondered how the story would end as I walked over Hollywood Boulevard. But you see there are plenty of characters there – you should try it some time and make notes.

There are ten million stories in the naked city."

****

15

Over the next few weeks it was a new Alfredo about the house. I don't know what he was going to do with the story from the bus but I could hear him getting out of bed most mornings at around six-o-clock. Then he would work till around eleven o clock and break for breakfast. I would meet him in the kitchen sometimes as I struggled through Patrick's one- sided conversation about baseball. He didn't seem to care about Alfredo's good news in fact he acted slightly different towards him as if he was jealous. After all he was the actor in the household and, before we came, was the Irishman too. He was so much of an Irishman that one day, as he was reading the newspaper, he asked Alfredo and me who Sean Finn was. Of course, neither of us knew who he was. "Call yourselves Irish?" Patrick said. "He's in all the newspapers. He's in negotiations about the cease-fire."

"Well he's new to me!" said Alfredo.

"What would you know" said Patrick "you're neither one thing nor the other."

"What do you mean?" I said

"He's Jewish!"

"Ah!" said Alfredo. "That's something you don't understand. There are two kinds of Jews in Ireland: the Catholic Jews and the Protestant Jews."

Patrick looked at him, not knowing whether it was a joke or not.

I grabbed the newspaper: "Who's this Sean Finn?" I said.

"There!"

"It's Sinn Fein" I said.

Alfredo and I laughed.

"I'll have to write about that" said Alfredo.

"It's Sinn Fein" I said to Patrick "that's how it's pronounced.

And I said it slowly phonetically "Shinn Fain."

"You're supposed to be an Irishman" said Alfredo, "but you're about as Irish as Betty's arse. Did you know Ireland is one of the few countries in the world that didn't persecute the Jews?"

"So?" said Patrick.

"So stop persecuting me y'owl bollix!"

The two of us laughed, and Patrick went off to take a shower mumbling something about telling the INS about Alfredo.

"They never persecuted us because they never let us in" he added under his breath to me.

Then he said "It's finished."

"The screenplay?"

"The very same."

"I'll read it tonight when I get back. Put a copy of it on my bed."

"I don't have a copy. You'll have to read it on the screen."

"Oh! Okay then."

"Now."

He took me into his room and I sat at the computer. He seemed a bit agitated and was wandering around the tiny room, looking out of the window and rubbing his hands together.

"Oh there's that woman with her kids" he said "she's beautiful. Come and look."

I went to him at the window and we could see a girl of about thirty walking with one child in a pushchair and one walking beside her. The one walking must have been about six years old.

"I think she's a single mother" he said "I never see her with a man."

"You like her?"

"Yes" he said, and started rubbing his chin "there's no way I can get to know her. That would be a ready-made family for me. But it'll never happen. I'm not like you. You just walk up to people and say hello. Me? I'm useless. I'll just have to continue fantasising about her."

As he said this he pointed to his bed.

I half expected him to ask me to go out and ask her for a date but he didn't. He just stood there looking quite sad as if he had nobody in the world; and he didn't really: except perhaps me.

"Come on" he said "get on with it."

What he didn't know was that I didn't know how to work the computer. This came as a bit of a shock to him as he didn't think there were any of us left. After he showed me how it worked I settled in for a good read and he went back to the kitchen to add even more ingredients to his oatmeal.

The first impression was that the screenplay wasn't very good. I could see the way he had written the dialogue and it impressed me the way he said so much with just a few words. When I was about twenty or so pages in to it, he came back with his oatmeal and, as usual, ate it straight from the saucepan.

"If you press any of the other letters on the keyboard" he said "don't worry about it. It doesn't matter unless you press save."

"Oh God" I said "where's save?"

"Don't worry about it." he said, and he went to the bathroom.

He was the usual hour in there and when he returned I had read about eighty percent.

"What do you think so far?"

"Rubbish." I said.

He laughed – he knew the Morecambe and Wise joke, I knew Morecambe and Wise but the Americans would never know them - then he started to put his big hiking boots on and get ready for a hike.

"I have to go" he said "I can't stand waiting here for you to finish."

He got himself ready and left me to read the screenplay. He took the floppy disc from the lap top before going and told me I was reading off the clip board and showed me how to turn the computer off.

As soon as he left, Patrick poked his head around the open door. He had a twinkle in his eye and a half smile on his face: "What's it like?" He said

"What?"

"The script; is it any good?"

"I like it" I said.

"Is there a role in it for me?"

"Yes there's an eejit at the beginning."

"No – seriously – is there anything for me?"

"You'll have to keep on the right side of Alfredo" I said "and he might write you into it."

"Could he do that?"

"You should try and get into his play reading about Joyce."

"Who's she?"

"James Joyce" I said "he's after an Irishman."

"I'm as Irish as Betty's arse" he said.

I laughed. He made me laugh. Things were looking up.

"He can create anything" I said "at the touch of his typewriter keys."

"I'll be damned" he said and slunk away.

He wasn't going to read anything. He was far too lazy. The truth was the screenplay wasn't very good. I was going to have to try and think how I could break it to Alfredo without hurting him. He had been so full of life for the preceding few weeks that I didn't want to put him down; he seemed to be obsessed with the workings of the woman's body. There was a thirty-year-old girl in the script who was the wife of the missing politician and in the screenplay she had at least three major references to her menstrual periods. Her periods were used as an excuse for declining invitations, for being late for an appointment and for dropping a bag of sugar at the supermarket. At the supermarket she had told the checkout girl that she was 'on the rag.' I didn't think this was suitable dialogue. I also wondered if he had based this character on the girl whom he had told me about earlier and was the object of some of his fantasies.

16

It was around ten that evening before I saw Alfredo again. As I came into the house I could hear Patrick's loud voice.

"You've got nothing to lose" he said.

He was sitting in the kitchen and Alfredo was standing.

"I have everything to lose" said Alfredo "I'm Jewish."

"I know but if you come to mass with me you'll have a foot in both camps."

I could see that Patrick was under the influence of vodka. It didn't seem to take much for him to let his mouth rip. He turned to me "This guy won't take a chance."

"I'll take a chance on a glass of vodka" I said, as I poured a large drink and went out into the garden.

I could still hear them from the back garden swing so I went to the deck by the guest house.

After a while Alfredo came out to me. He climbed the few steps to the top of the deck and looked up at the stars.

"There was a philosopher called Pascal" he said.

He turned to me: "You've heard of him?"

I shrugged. I hadn't.

"A seventeenth century Frenchman who said that it was worth betting that God existed; the chances are very small but the reward is great if you win: that's Patrick – I just told him; he's betting on the existence of the after life. What he doesn't realise is that you have to truly believe to be accepted in heaven. God knows what goes on in your head: you can't hedge your bets."

"You believe in God?"

"Yes" he said "and I reject science. I don't believe in science."

"You don't believe in science? What do you mean?"

"They have it wrong! They're so fucking arrogant in their theories and fucking experiments; and trying to invent drugs to make us live forever, on the one hand, and trying to invent weapons that will annihilate us on the other."

He laughed then looked at the stars for a few minutes.

"Not very good is it?" he said "The screenplay?"

I shrugged; he continued to look at the stars: "The fault, dear Brutus, is not in our stars."

"What do you mean?" I said.

"Julius Caesar! I'm after the truth; it's not very good. I've lost my talent and it's my fault. It's all gone. I need to get a job as a nursing assistant and do something useful with my life."

We didn't speak for a few moments; but it was comfortable; it wasn't awkward.

"Maybe I'll just write the treatment and forget the screenplay."

"What did Patrick say when you told him about Pascal?"

"It went in one ear and out the other. He's been very nice to me, though, for some reason."

"He wants a part in your movie" I said "How are you getting on with the James Joyce play?"

A strange look came over his face: "I know what you're thinking" he said.

"What?"

"You are thinking that my James Joyce play will be a load of rubbish too."

"No I'm not" and I meant it.

"Do you want to read it? What I've written so far?"

"How much have you written?"

"About thirty pages."

"Yes" I said.

"I'll give you a copy tomorrow."

"Okay."

"Wants a part in my movie, does he?"

He laughed and went back into the house leaving me to contemplate the stars and look for the truth.

Five minutes later Patrick came out with the bottle of vodka.

"Alfredo said he will get me into his movie" he said rather incoherently as he refreshed my glass.

"He said I'm too old to play James Joyce. Do you want some ice?"

I nodded and he tipped some from a glass he was balancing. As he tipped it some of his drink poured onto the floor.

"Steady" I said.

We stayed till we finished the bottle; he was pleasant enough to drink with but he was prejudiced and racist. However, it was a good drink and something I needed; it meant that I didn't take care of the dishes so at the crack of dawn the next day the banging started. Patrick had used every piece of cooking utensil from the kitchen, and Alfredo had helped to make the largest pile of dishes ever. This might have been behind my decision to ignore the chore but because the stack was so big it took Betty a long time to throw the dishes into the cupboard a few inches from where I was trying to sleep. Then the banging stopped and I turned over, hopefully, to finish my sleep. This was the cue for the local leaf blower to start and I gave up the idea of going back to sleep as a bad one.

I decided to call my mother in Dublin but as soon as I put the phone to my ear I could hear there was no dialling tone. I said "Hello?"

"Hello" came from the other end and into my ear.

It was Betty with her morning call.

"What are you doing up?"

"Are you kidding?" I said. "There's more noise here than Piccadilly Circus."

"He's borrowed money from Patrick."

"Who Alfredo?"

"Yes."

"How do you know?"

"Patrick told me."

"When?"

"Just now; before he went for his walk.

"How much?"

"He didn't say. Alfredo hasn't paid any rent since he moved in."

"Have you tackled him about it?"

"No."

"No? Why not?"

"I just . . I was wondering whether you could ask him."

"I can't, Betty" I said "it's none of my business."

As I put the phone down I saw Alfredo's script, which had been pushed under my door. I did feel sorry for Betty.

****

17

It wasn't finished but it was brilliant. It was very hard to believe that the same person who wrote the screenplay had written the beautiful piece of work that I was reading. I learned a lot about James Joyce, his wife Nora and a lot about schizophrenia in just thirty pages. The more I read it, though, the more I could truly see that it was written by the same man who wrote the screenplay about the politician. The screenplay about the politician was awful but I could see it had been written by a professional doing a job. The play about James Joyce was written from the heart and with care and understanding; it was a piece of art as opposed to using writing as a craft.

At around eleven o clock I heard Alfredo coming through the front door. He came into the kitchen with a few bags of groceries and deposited two gallons of ice cream into the freezing section of the fridge and a large jar of apple juice into the fridge proper.

Then he went back into the living room; he had been to the library and had drawn out about ten books or so and they were in a pile just inside the front door; next to the books he had bought, probably, about twenty CDs.

"I had to go to the bank" he said, as he picked up the books and CDs.

So it was true. He had borrowed the money.

"Why did you buy two cartons?"

"One's frozen yoghurt" he replied "I need fuel to work. I gotta do another draft of the screenplay."

"And the CDs and books?

"I need them."

"What happened to the idea of getting a job as a nursing assistant?"

"I'll finish the screenplay first. Then I'm going to write about a young girl called Gertie who goes to the west of Ireland in search of a husband. I got the idea the night of the Bloomsday Blackout; that young girl on stage showing us her drawers and saying her lines so quietly; and that gobshite of a newspaper critic telling her to speak up: the stupid bowsey of a bearded bastard!"

He laughed at what he had said.

"That describes him doesn't it? 'The stupid bowsey of a bearded bastard!' I'll write that down."

He took a pencil from his pocket and wrote the phrase.

"Is that where you keep it all?" I asked.

"There you are – look!"

He showed me the piece of paper. He had also scribbled 'Pascal, betting on the after life existing.'

"Will you go back to Ireland to write?"

"Write what?"

"About Gertie."

"Don't need to go anywhere," he said "maybe a mental hospital. A writer carries his country around in his head."

Then he went back to his room.

A few minutes later he came back and, without saying a word, took one of the cartons of ice cream out of the freezer and into his room. I heard his door close hard and then there was silence for a while.

I rinsed my cup and got into the shower. When I got out I could hear loud music coming from his room. Loud hippy type music from the nineteen sixties or seventies! I think it was Crosby, Stills and Nash; I wasn't sure as I wasn't much of a fan.

It was still playing when I left the house. I knocked on his door as I passed it to say goodbye and he shouted 'working' as I went out.

****

18

I didn't see Alfredo for a few days. He stayed in bed in the mornings till around eleven and got straight on with his work when he got up. Then he would go to the bathroom for the usual hour with Patrick's Los Angeles Times and go out for his walk.

Sometimes he'd take the dog and sometimes he would leave it to cry after him. I figured he wanted a rest from my optimistic cheerfulness so I let it go at that. I was left to the usual routine of listening to Betty's telephone messages and snippets of the O.J. Simpson murder trial. One of Betty's messages was to say that Patrick had made Alfredo promise to pay him back before he paid Betty the rent and there was no reason to disbelieve her.

One day I was sitting with Betty and Patrick at the kitchen table and Patrick's telephone rang. When he answered it he took the phone with him up to his room and came down later with a subdued smile on his face. By this time Betty had retreated into the garden using the usual safety antenna, which made her disappear if she thought she would have to confront anything. Maybe she thought Patrick was about to take some bad news but it wasn't bad news he was about to tell me.

"I got it" he said.

"What?"

"Alimony!"

"What do you mean?"

"I got three thousand a month alimony from my wife; thanks to you taking the pictures."

It had never crossed my mind that he was the one after alimony. I thought that he was trying to make himself look poor to avoid big payments. His wife was the breadwinner of the family and he had sued her to keep him in the style of living he was used to.

"Have you had breakfast yet?"

"No."

"Come on" he said "they do a champagne brunch at Gloria's on Sundays. Maybe they'll do one for us today?"

So we went to Gloria's and he persuaded them to prepare the champagne brunch. It was a place I liked with its running water fountains and friendly staff and it was only a few yards walk down Maltman on the corner of Sunset.

"Where's Betty?" said the waiter.

"Where's Betty!" said Patrick and shrugged.

"She's gardening" I said.

"Doing yard work" said Patrick.

"Why does she sweep the street on Monday mornings?" asked the waiter.

Patrick laughed.

"What's that?" I asked.

"You need to get out of bed in the mornings" said Patrick, and then to the waiter: "It's her contribution to the community."

"She found a small bag of cocaine last week" said the waiter.

"You see what you miss by staying in bed?" Patrick said to me.

"I'll have to start getting up early." I replied.

The waiter left two menus and went away.

It was a wonderful brunch and Patrick told me he would now look for an apartment in Beverly Hills and asked me if I wanted to move in with him. I wasn't sure how to take this and the phrase 'move in with him' seemed to have other connotations.

"We can have a great time together." he said, "We can go to Dan

Tanna's, that club on Le Cienega, have breakfast out most mornings. I'll pay. You can use the Lexis."

It seemed a bit fishy to me. I didn't think he was gay so maybe he had a fatherly affection for me. Alfredo had always thought it was an homosexual affection but I had never given it more than that passing thought as he was a married man with children and grandchildren; in any case Alfredo was strange when it came to families; so far he hadn't mentioned his own and evaded the subject each time I asked.

When I rejected Patrick's offer I could see he was offended.

"I'll never ask you again" he said, as we walked back to Betty's.

19

I could hear that Alfredo was in his room. I knocked, gently, and went in. He was sitting at his desk, under the place where he slept, and I could see by his eyes that he had been crying. He stopped crying when I went in and asked me to sit down.

This was difficult as the only place to sit in his room was where he was.

"Let me get a chair" I said, and I went back to my room to get one.

His eyes were quite dry, when I got back, but very bloodshot. He was wearing khaki shorts, a San Francisco bicycle tee shirt and was bare footed. The tee shirt didn't exactly say San Francisco. It was to commemorate a bicycle race in nineteen ninety-one: the words said 'Tour of San France Cisco' and there was a picture of a bicycle; at first glance it looked like 'Tour de France' as the 'San' and the 'Cisco' were written in white on different coloured backgrounds.
In the corner of the room there was a plastic bag of soda cans and plastic bottles.

"What's with the tee shirt?" I said.

"I have lost everybody," he said. "I have no money, no talent, I'm losing you and…" he took a very deep breath when his voice started to break. I could see he was struggling to control his emotions: "I'm on my uppers. I have nothing. No money, no talent and no prospects. I collected a few coke cans to take to the recycling centre."

He gestured at the cans in the corner.

"Why don't you sell the banjo?"

"I wouldn't sell the banjo. You play it."

"If you need money you should sell the banjo no matter who plays it. Take it to one of the guitar shops on Sunset; up by Gardner."

"I'm not selling the banjo" he said finally.

He turned to face his computer as if he was waiting for a message of what he was to write next.

"I was in this bicycle race in ninety-one," he said, patting his chest: "I wasn't always two hundred and fifty pounds, you know."

"How much is two hundred and fifty pounds?"

"About sixteen stone" he replied "I used to ride around Marin County. I'd go as far as Stinson Beach. Cycle all the way up there from San Francisco, I would. I knew a girl and we would cycle together and when we got there we would lie on the sand and let our cares float out on the Pacific Ocean. Then we would have a picnic on the sand and she would fix sandwiches for me.

The tears had gone and even the redness was disappearing from his eyes as he turned to me: "You should go to Stinson Beach" he said "take a good woman with you. Have you ever been to San Francisco?"

"Yes."

"Have you ever stayed there for any length of time?"

"Couple of days."

"You should go to San Francisco" he said "you should go and stay and experience the Haight-Ashbury thing; it's all gone now, but even so. Just spend a couple of days there so you'll know where Haight-Ashbury is and where it was;

then go to Marin County and stay for a whole year. I was there for five years. I had my plays produced at the theatre. That's where I started writing my play on Joyce."

"It's beautiful" I said "what's happening with it?"

"It's going on at the Egyptian Arena for a public reading."

"When?"

"When and if I finish it. I want you to come."

His room fell silent for a few seconds and I could hear the ticking.

"I want you to play James Joyce."

"I don't think so."

There was a pause.

"I need to work" he said then he burst into life and grabbed me by the shoulder.

"Come on, out you go" he said.

He started shoving me. I could feel his soft hands on my shoulders. He shoved me very hard but I held my ground and shoved back. He shoved harder but I wasn't giving way. We were soon in the immovable object meeting the irresistible force theory.

"We're going to break something" he said.

"OK."

"OK."

And we let each other go. I picked up my chair.

"I want nothing negative" I said as I left the room.

I went back to my room and picked up the James Joyce partly written script from my bed. I took it back to him. He was sitting at his desk when I got back to his room.

"Thank you for the privilege" I said as I handed the pages to him.

20

One day I found a business card on my bed. It was from Betty's boy friend, Harold. He'd written on it 'I would not like to lose contact.'

He took Betty everywhere at weekends. Maybe he liked to be seen with a famous television star even though she had left the soap opera some years earlier. Once in a while they would arrive home and she would say "The paparazzi were there tonight! They saw me coming."

It reminded me of Norma Desmond from 'Sunset Boulevard.' I could imagine Betty posing for their photographs and enjoying every minute of the attention. I had never seen her in the soap opera and neither had Alfredo. Patrick had seen it as he had told me about it when I first arrived at the house.

He was always on the look out for women to date and one evening he took a casting director, who was Betty's friend, out dancing.

Another thing he would do was to place advertisements in the 'Men seeking Women' column of the LA Weekly. His phone would ring a lot when he did this, as Los Angeles can be a lonely place for the single person. I didn't let it bother me, as I was on an adventure looking for a killing even though I didn't know what kind of killing I was after. Besides I had plenty of female company at work and once in a while I would take one of them out.

Patrick didn't tell Betty that he had advertised, but would make it very obvious when a woman rang, that it was a romantic liaison on the other end of the line if she was in the same room. He was trying to make her jealous.

"He's doing well" she would say when he would take his cordless phone from the room.

I didn't think it was any of my business so I didn't tell her. I would have loved to see his advertisements to see how he described himself.

I told Betty about Harold's card "Oh he just wanted you to know where he was in case you needed him" she said "he likes you. I hear you went to Gloria's with Patrick."

"How did you know?"

"I have a friend who works there."

She told me that she would see Harold at the weekends and somebody else, from Gloria's, during the week. That was where she would disappear to each evening.

The pile of soda cans and plastic water bottles piled up in the back of Alfredo's car over the next week adding to the pile in the corner of his room.

In the back garden he had filled the clothesline with his wet laundry and everything, as usual, had been dumped on it with no clothes pegs or anything else to make sure the laundry stayed where it was. He had also dumped some suitcases onto the front porch and all of this became the subjects of Betty's morning telephone messages.

One day he came into my room and put a piece of paper in front of me:

'Man Seeking Woman over Forty for companionship and SEX.'

I looked at it for a few minutes and said "Is this another commission from the Schlepper?"

"No" he said "that's me! What do you think?"

"What's it for? The LA Weekly?"

"Yes."

"Did you get the idea from Patrick?"

"No. He got the idea from me. I've been doing it for years in different towns. It's what I prefer. What do you think?"

"I'm not sure whether you should put for sex?"

"Why not? It's what I want."

I couldn't believe that anybody would answer it.

"I talk to them on the phone and, eventually, we meet up. I told some of them in the past to park in a certain street, and then I would drive up, get into the car and fuck them."

"And fuck off?"

"And fuck off" he replied "Sometimes we wouldn't even speak. I'll take this into the LA Weekly tomorrow when I take the cans to be recycled."

" Betty wants the rubbish moved from the front porch?"

"Maybe she should ask; I'll do anything she asks." he said "Do you want to come to the recycling place with me tomorrow? I'll take you into work: save you catching the bus."

"If there's room in the car – but I'm not working tomorrow."

21

The recycling place was somewhere near the end of Santa Monica Boulevard; it was where the down and outs, alcoholics, mentally ill, homeless and part time insolvents, like Alfredo, took their used soda cans, plastic bottles and newspapers to redeem the duty paid. Hardly anybody else turned up in a car, as the usual mode of delivery was a supermarket-shopping cart. It was a ridiculous state of affairs and, sometimes, the only income for the old, infirm and homeless.

The shopping carts were used against the permission of the supermarkets and on many occasions were seized back by, what can only be described as, supermarket shopping cart bounty hunters.

These people would drive around in pick-up trucks scouring the streets of Los Angeles for carts, which they would collect and take back to the supermarkets for a reward.

Most of the time they would find them outside apartment buildings, where shoppers had wheeled their groceries home and dumped the carts in the street. Sometimes nasty supermarket shopping cart bounty hunters would see a person with a cart full of soda cans, plastic bottles and the like, and take the cart from them spilling the contents into the street. This would involve a lot of shouting and screaming but the bullies would always win which usually left the down and out, alcoholic, homeless or mentally ill person sitting on the kerb in tears and frustration looking at their hard work lying in the street and their entire possessions scattered around. Some of the homeless would hide their bags and other belongings in hedges at the side of the street because of this but would have to secret the bag there when there was nobody about. Once in a while the police would seize a supermarket-shopping cart and tip the contents into the street too charging the person in possession with theft.

The day we arrived at the recycling centre the yard had just been cleaned with a hosepipe and there were bits of wet newspaper on the floor, making it very slippery. A very big bare footed black man was sweeping the excess water into a drain.

"Look at him" said Alfredo.

"Who?"

"Your man: the big black fella. He was in that hotel on Highland I was staying at. He would go up to people in the street and say 'Hey man! I just come out of the penitentiary. Can you help a brother out?"

"That's what you said to me when we first met."

"When?"

"That night outside the hotel in Highland."

He laughed "I was rehearsing" he said.

"For what?"

"I was going to Hollywood Boulevard to stick my hand out; I was practising on you."

"Did you make any money?"

"No! I never had the guts to do it."

The big man kept sweeping and we looked at him.

"Look at the poor bastard" he said "every time he gets to a traffic light and sees the sign to 'walk' – he walks. It's the only right he feels he has."

We pulled up in the yard and, as we got out of the car, there were a couple of supermarket shopping carts being wheeled in. One of them was so full with plastic bags of bottles hanging from various parts of the cart that the man, who had pushed it through the streets in the hot sunshine of California, just flopped down exhausted staring at the floor as if he couldn't believe that his long push had come to an end. He lifted his head to look at the load knowing that as soon as it was emptied from the cart he would start the long process again of filling and pushing it back. After a few breaths of recovery, he lit a small cigarette and reached for one of the bottles drinking its contents in one enormous gulp.

I helped Alfredo unload the car then sat back inside it to wait for him to complete his transaction.

He came out of the office with a huge smile on his face and when he got into the car he showed me his money:

"Eight dollars" he said

He clapped his other hand onto it, and put it into the bag on his belt to keep his floppy discs company.

22

The following weekend Alfredo's phone rang off the hook. In fact his phone rang from the moment the LA Weekly came out on the Thursday till Sunday evening. It started early in the morning till late at night. There was obviously a lot of forty something females who wanted Alfredo's body. But there again, they hadn't seen it.

In due course he was talking to about three of them and then ultimately to one and he talked to the one for hours at a time. I don't know if they were having phone sex or intellectual conversations as I stayed as far from his door as I could for fear of hearing any of it.

One day he came into my room and told me the woman he had chosen was coming around to the house "How do I look?"

He looked his usual self but instead of the khaki shorts and walking boots he was wearing a blue tracksuit bottom, blue tee shirt and a pair of flips-flops. The flip-flops were the kind that threaded through the big toe. He had combed his hair forward. I don't think he put anything on it apart from water so I suppose it would have dried but it looked ridiculous. He looked like a lost and aging Beatle. I tried to mess it up a little.

"No no no don't do that" he said, and started combing it forward again. Then he went back into his room and started brushing it forward.

"Why do you do that?"

"I like it like that" he said "makes me look good."

"Makes you look weird" I said.

"Will you open the door to her?

"Yes okay" I said.

That was it for me; I decided there and then that I would be going out that evening and freshened myself up ready to go.

A huge green car travelled slowly up the street and passed the house. Then it stopped and stayed where it was for a little while. I could see some movement inside and then the car travelled backwards till the front bumper came level with the drive. It was a Chevy Nova, maybe from about nineteen seventy-three, and when it stopped on the drive I waited with anticipation for her to get out; but she didn't. Maybe she was freshening herself up or having second thoughts. As I looked through the window I heard Alfredo go out of his back door and into the bathroom.

She was wearing a red sun hat and before she locked the driver's door she struggled with a tiny parasol. When it was extended she locked the car door then tried each of the other doors before walking to the front door of the house. I opened it before she knocked.

"Oh" she said "you were looking out for me."

"I sure was" I said.

I smiled.

"I'm Leah."

"Come in" I said.

She wiped her feet and struggled again with the parasol: this time to fold it up. I took it from her and put it into the umbrella rack that stood just inside the door.

She smiled at me.

"Is my car okay there?" she said.

I could tell she was from Boston by the way she said car: Caaaaaaaaaar!

"I thought you said you had white hair" she said.

"Ah but I'm not Alfredo" I said "he is lurking behind that door."

I pointed to it but I knew he wasn't; I knew he was in the can plastering his hair forward.

"Would you like to sit down?"

"Yes" she said.

There was a big cloth over the sofa and I removed some of it to let her sit; as I did so, a huge spider ran out and hid behind the cushions; she didn't see it.

"Lurking?" she said.

"Lurking." I said.

I liked her she seemed to have a sense of humour and would be good for Alfredo.

"He's in the bathroom I think."

"Lovely house." she said, looking around.

"Yes" I said. "Can I get a drink for you? Water? Tea?"

"No thank you" she said.

So where was Alfredo? Was he 'doing a Betty' and disappearing at the precise moment of confrontation? 'I fuck them in the car then I fuck off!' In his mind, he did.

"You're the gentleman who works at the Hollywood Bowl" she said.

"Gentleman!" I said "I like that."

"I want to make you feel secure:" she said.

There was a kind of a wink of the eye in her voice.

A moment of silence:

"I'll get some tickets for you if you want. Let me know when you can go."

She didn't take the red sun hat off so it was hard to see what kind of woman she was. She wore big red and white striped pantaloons under a long light coat.

"That's very kind" she said.

"What are you doing in this part of the world?"

"My children are here" she said "I want to be near them!"

Then she smiled, put her head to one side and sat on the sofa with her hands folded in her lap as if she was having pleasant thoughts about her children.

"Excuse me for a moment" I said.

I walked around the passageway to my room. The bathroom door was shut and so was Alfredo's door. I was ready to go out for the evening so I checked to see if all was okay in my room and went back around to Leah in the living room.

"He won't be a moment" I said optimistically.

"I'm part Irish." she said "I'm one half Irish, one fourth Scotch and one-fourth Cherokee Indian."

"The Scots will kill you if you call them Scotch."

"I know" she said "but they would be wrong. If you look at the old books you will see that they are referred to as Scotch: the Scotch. They say Scotch is a whisky but whisky is whisky. If you ask for a Scotch in polite society you will be wrong: in London for example."

She looked at the Van Erp lamp; she almost lost her breath.

"Look at that" she said.

"What - the lamp?"

"Yes" she said "beautiful!"

"It could be." I said.

"Does she know how much it's worth?"

"I don't know" I said.

She gave it a good look without touching it.

"You look what I thought Alfredo sounded like. In fact you sound a bit like him."

"I look like him too" I said "he's me with white hair."

I laughed.

"Really?"

I shook my head.

"People here think that the Irish are red headed. But they're not – they're like me."

"Black Irish:" she said.

I could hear Alfredo entering his room.

"Excuse me" I said.

I went to his back door, rapped on it and went in. He was rubbing his wet hands together nervously. This time he had combed his hair across with a parting just above his right ear. He couldn't even part his hair in a good place.

"What are you doing?"

"I had to go just in case" he whispered "what's she like?"

I grabbed his comb and tried to straighten his parting.

"Straightening my parting?" he said.

"Come and look." I went back to Leah but he didn't follow me.

"Here he is" I said thinking he was behind me but he wasn't.

"Come on" I called.

Nothing happened; I looked at Leah; she smiled and I shrugged; then he awkwardly looked around the door; he had combed his hair forward again.

"Come on" I said.

He came into the room.

"I'll leave you to it."

"You're right" she said.

I looked at her.

"He's nothing like you."

I wasn't sure what he was going to do with her or even to her but he had advertised for sex and I didn't want to be anywhere near the house, let alone his room, if and when, it happened so I walked down to the Vista on Sunset Boulevard to see a movie.

23

She was long gone by the time I got back. I could hear his television when I entered the house and I didn't want to know anything. Leah must have been around sixty years of age, maybe more, and I just didn't want to imagine her doing anything or hear anything from Alfredo about what she had been doing or any of his sexual exploits real or imagined. It was okay to hear about him getting into cars for quick sex when I couldn't put a face to the female but since I had met Leah I didn't want to know anything.

When I saw him the next day he didn't mention anything at all. Patrick and Betty were away as it was Sunday and I decided to ignore Betty's telephone message for the day and wipe it before playing it back. I knew what it would be: he hadn't paid the rent, the clothes were still on the line and the rubbish was still on the porch: the garbage, as she called it. Actually it consisted of three leather suitcases, which was hardly garbage. His clothes had been on the line for two weeks. He had put them there the day before he put the advertisement into the LA Weekly and there we were with his advertisement published, the blind date fulfilled and in spite of everything his clothes hanging there like monsters in the night. He came into the kitchen as I was contemplating moving from the chair to make coffee.

"Good morning" I said.

He seemed a bit smug but didn't say anything straight away.

"What's happening?"

"Nothing" I said "I was thinking I might go out for breakfast."

"Getting very American; going out for breakfast!"

"Better than cooking it then having to wash up afterwards."

"You should be like me" he said "and eat from the pot: cuts one chore out in a stroke."

"Yes but I'm not a savage like you."

He used Patrick's filtered water to add to his oats then he went through his usual modus operandi of putting in as many herbs as possible. He had started to pronounce herbs without sounding the aitch as the Americans do.

"You're the one who's getting American 'erb.'"

"Only when I'm working."

"Working?"

"The Schlepper wants the treatment by tomorrow."

"The treatment? I thought you were doing a screenplay!"

"No. He called on Friday to say that he is paying for a treatment and that's all he wants. So that's all I'll write. We'll write my screenplay later and cut him out of the picture."

"We?"

"Yes. You and me! Can you cash a cheque for me?"

"Yes" I said.

"Good. He'll pay me tomorrow morning and he might make the cheque to cash but in case he won't do that I'll get him to make it payable to you."

"Okay" I said "you can take me to the bank in the morning and I'll give you the cash."

"Don't you have to wait for it to clear?"

"I'll trust him." I said.

"Listen," he said "don't trust anybody."

"I can take it from my account and then we can knock fuck out of him if the cheque bounces."

He liked this; it made him laugh. I was going to give him all I had in the world at that moment but it was Alfredo I trusted not the Schlepper.

24

I was looking forward to seeing the Schlepper as Alfredo decided to take me in to see him whilst he delivered the treatment and collected the cheque. My image idea of a Hollywood producer in a plush office was dashed as we walked up a dingy staircase on Hollywood Boulevard, somewhere between Ivar and Cahuenga. When we entered the building the first thing I noticed was the smell: it was a mixture of cat's piss, skunk and age. On a wall plaque there were names of the film production companies, theatrical and model agencies that inhabited the building. It was hard to see after the very bright Hollywood Boulevard. It got lighter when our eyes got used to it and I could see that the names of the *Talent Agencies* and film companies showed a certain lack of imagination with names like Ajax, Apex, Acme and names that I had only seen in American comics before.

As we approached the Schlepper's door we could smell his cigar. Alfredo screwed up his nose.

The office was tiny with loads of papers, files, photographs and scripts strewn about it and the smell of cigars was worse inside. On the wall were movie posters and photographs of the Schlepper with minor celebrities of the day and yesterday. There were also photographs of semi nude adult movie-stars.

He struggled to find chairs for us both to sit in, even though I said it would be okay if I stood. We were only delivering a treatment after all.

Alfredo gave the treatment to the Schlepper, which he had put into a post office express mail envelope. The Schlepper took the treatment from the envelope and gave the envelope back to Alfredo.

"Okay Alf" he said "I'll cut you a cheque."

Alfredo explained that he wanted the cheque made out to me not requesting cash at all.

"I owe the sonofabitch!" he said.

He looked towards me and narrowed his eyes a little.

"Okay by me" said the Schlepper.

He wrote the cheque and handed it to me. I gave it to Alfredo, who checked the amount then handed it back to me. I put it into my shirt pocket. The Schlepper looked at this little pantomime and laughed: "I like you guys" he said as he chomped on his stogie.

****

25

We parked the car underneath the Wells Fargo Bank on Sunset Boulevard and I went up to the bank to deposit the cheque and get his money. It took a few minutes as there was a small queue but when I got back down to the car park Alfredo had gone.

"He wouldn't turn the engine off. We had to ask him to go!" said the attendant.

So there he was waiting in the little street outside with the engine ticking over as if he was a bank robber waiting for a quick getaway. His car was filling the street with carbon dioxide and it was starting to look like a foggy day.

"Here we are" I said.

I counted out seven hundred and fifty dollars into his hand. He clapped his other hand over it, as he had done at the recycling centre, and stuffed it into his pouch.

"Why didn't you wait?"

"If I stop the engine it might not start again. The son of a bitch told me to get out that I was poisoning him. I think I need a new battery."

26

We had to go to Pep Boys on Hollywood Boulevard, to buy the battery. At least some of the money wouldn't be going on ice cream and applesauce!

"I got another little job" he said as he drove.

"Yes?"

"Leah is an antique dealer and wants me to help her."

"Do what?"

"Just generally; she goes to the flea market at Pasadena Rose Bowl one Sunday a month and wants some help."

"Well done" I said.

"I'll be able to hold my head up for a change. I'll be able to pay my way. I'm looking forward to it."

When they told us at Pep Boys that we would have to wait for a while I said I would walk home and I asked Alfredo to look out for me on his way.

It was a very hot August day and halfway home I regretted my decision to walk. I regretted it even more when I got home, as I was so dehydrated I just flopped down on to the porch swing. It must have taken over an hour and I was surprised to see that Alfredo's car was nowhere in sight. I was also sure I could still smell the stink of the Schlepper's cigar.

Betty came out "Have you seen Alfredo?

I wasn't sure what to say, as I didn't want to let her know he had some money; it was none of my business.

"Why?"

"Somebody came to see him."

"Oh?"

"I can still smell his cigar" she said.

The Schlepper! I wondered what he wanted but I didn't have the energy to care.

"Unusual for you to take a morning walk" she said "you should come with us again."

"No thanks" I said "I've learned my lesson."

She went inside and came out with a glass of water for me.

When I came in that night Patrick was burning papers in the barbecue on the porch. Betty was sitting on the porch swing, holding papers, and when the flame died down she handed Patrick more.

"Won't you ruin the barbecue burning paper like that?" I said.

"No" said Patrick "I usually start it with paper."

He squirted lighter fuel onto the residue and it flared up. Then I noticed that Alfredo's door was open.

"What are you burning?"

"Not going to be any movie." said Patrick.

"What are you talking about?"

"His producer came here today; said your friend had written a load of shit and he wants his money back - threatened us because we wouldn't let him in to the house. So I'm not going to be in the movie! Boy that was a waste!"

"What?" I said "Who said you were going to be in the movie?"

"You said yourself he creates characters with his keyboard."

He reached across to a piece of paper that was set apart.

"Look at this" he said: he read out loud: "Patrick, betting on the after life existing. The stupid bowsey of a beaded bastard! What does he think I am - a hippy?"

"Hang on" I said "you've got no right to go through his papers."

"He's not going to write about me" said Patrick "I'm not gonna let him."

"He's not writing about you. Who would want to write about you?"

I snatched the paper from him.

"Look" I said "it says Pascal not Patrick; and bearded not beaded."

He snatched the paper back, looked at it in confusion and threw it onto the dying fire. Alfredo's scribbled words burst into flame. I knew Alfredo had everything important on floppy disc so it wouldn't be a big deal to him but the principle disturbed me. I wandered into his room and could see that his lap top computer was missing; the cable was still plugged into the wall and the end flopped pathetically over the side of Alfredo's desk like a headless snake. Propped up next to it, on his big dial telephone, was an envelope with Patrick's handwriting on it.

I went back out to the porch. Betty was gone; it figured.

"What do you mean? 'Who would want to write about me?'"

"What I say! Who would want to write about an estate agent? You're nothing. Doing something like this is beneath contempt."

"We are what made America great; the great middle class!"

"The silent majority."

"Yes the silent majority. Anybody would write about me if they knew me and if they could write."

"Nobody would write about a character like you" I said "nobody in their right mind. They'd have to change you so drastically just to give you a tiny bit of charisma that it wouldn't be worth trying!"

He poked the burning paper and it frizzled into orange and red patterns in the barbecue, my observation rolling off him like water off a duck's back.

"Fuck off" I said, and I walked inside.

I told him to fuck off nearly every evening so this wouldn't come as any surprise.

I couldn't see where Betty was which was just as well or I might have said the same to her. There was going to be an explosion later on and she had disappeared, probably to Gloria's.

On my bed was a letter from Dublin and it was relaxing to read it. Reading a letter from a real person about real and important things relaxed me and took me, temporarily, out of the mad house of the existence I was in.

Eventually I went out to the porch closing Alfredo's door as I passed it. I sat there swinging to and fro, looking at the little bits of traffic passing and the stars starting to appear in the sky; the one or two people walking up the street, taking their dogs up to the grassy knoll at the top for a crap and watching them walk down again with their dogs walking easier and the dog walkers carrying bags of shit; listening to the sound of cop cars in the distance and the helicopters in the sky and wondering what my mother would make of all this and thinking of my sister in Dublin who had just written giving me the great news that she was pregnant and telling me that everybody but everybody at home was delighted as if I didn't think they would be; telling me a joke that nobody here would understand so I wouldn't be telling anybody, not even Alfredo, and asking me if I would ever be coming home. I let that thought sink into my head and asked myself the same question as I watched the paper fire die; I poked it dead to make sure it was gone.

I didn't see Alfredo drive up. He just appeared as if from nowhere carrying two bags of groceries and wearing the usual big smile.

"Enjoy the walk?" he said as he went in to the house.

I put two fingers up to him and he laughed. When he had planted the groceries he came back out and gave me the finger: "We're in America, now" he said and went back in.

I got up and went to my room to wait for the inevitable reaction. It came in the form of a very loud bang from Alfredo's room. It sounded as if he had broken something and as I was walking towards his door there was another bang, which seemed even louder. When I reached him he was sitting at his desk and he turned to face me blood streaming down his face. He had banged his head on the desk. In his hand was the opened envelope.

"You betrayed me" he said.

"What?"

"Look at this! Look!"

He thrust the contents of the envelope at me. I looked at the piece of paper, which was an invoice from Patrick for six hundred dollars.

"What's this about?"

His eyes were as red as the blood streaming down his face and on to his chin. I picked up a tissue and tried to mop the blood. He grabbed it from my hand and threw it violently on to the floor.

"What do you think it is? Look at this!"

He referred to the letter.

"Steady" I said "steady!"

"How did he know I was paid today if you didn't tell him?"

"You borrowed six hundred dollars?" I said.

"How did he know I was paid today if you didn't tell him?" he repeated.

"I've just walked in not half an hour ago" I said "The Schlepper was here demanding his money back. Said you wrote a piece of shite."

"The Schlepper was here when you came back?"

"No he'd been here earlier."

He looked at the paper and then glared at me again.

"Did he take my computer? If he's taken my computer I'll kill the fucker. I'll kill the motherfucker!"

"Hang on hang on: they didn't let him in."

"Then Patrick's got it" he said.

He rose out of his chair and tried to get passed me. I stood my ground.

"Let me pass" he said "I don't want to hurt you."

"I'm not moving."

He tried to push me, gently, aside but I stood my ground. Soon we were in the immovable object and irresistible force situation again.

"I'm not moving" I said.

"Nor me. Is Patrick in his room?"

"I think so."

As I said that he gave a really sudden push and nearly toppled me.

"What are you going to do" I said "hit him with your banjo?"

This made him smile.

"Get the blood off your face and I'll go up to him?"

He relaxed.

"Off of your face" he mimicked.

"I didn't say that!"

"I know" he said "God why do we even bother?"

"They burned your papers too."

He smiled "What for?"

"Patrick said you were writing about him."

He laughed at this. "So I join the ranks of the immortals."

"Sit down and I'll go up."

"Only a little fella you are" he called out as I left his room "but you held me."

I smiled as I climbed the stairs knowing full well that if he'd have gone totally berserk, nothing would have held him.

I could hear Patrick talking on the telephone when I got to his door; I knocked it hard in any case.

"Hold it" he shouted.

"Okay."

Presently he came to the door "What was all the noise?"

"Nothing" I said.

"I was gonna call the cops."

"Shut up" I said as I walked in and stood in the doorway "What did you expect?"

"Wouldn't write about me, huh?"

"What did you expect" I repeated "You burn his papers and take his computer. Where is it?"

"Betty took it in lieu of rent."

"Betty? I said "With your encouragement, I suppose. Well she doesn't have the right. Where is it?"

"I don't know."

He put his hand to the door ready to close it. I could see he had consumed a few glasses of vodka, something I wouldn't be doing with him again.

"I'm busy" he said and went to close the door.

"Fuck you" I said and turned to leave.

He flicked the door closed and it caught the heel of my shoe as I was leaving. I opened the door again flinging it back violently. It made a loud cracking noise on the closet. At this he took a quick step back and fell onto the bed breaking the cross piece of the footboard as he fell. I think this convinced him, at last, that I was serious.

I carried on down the stairs to Alfredo. He was sitting at the desk.

"Have some ice cream" I said "and I'll look for your computer."

I went out of his room but he followed me. The first place I went to was the cantina underneath the kitchen. I turned the light on as I went in and the same old smell and fascination hit me.

"Holy shite" said Alfredo "what a place; I'm going to come and sit in here."

I looked around but couldn't see the computer.

"Come on" I said.

He followed me to the other door, which was underneath my room, and as soon as I opened it the lap top computer was the first thing I saw.

"Thank fuck the Schlepper didn't take it" he said "I would have had to kill him."

"Is it okay?"

"Yes." he said.

We went to sit on the deck by the guesthouse; Alfredo opened the computer and turned it on to see if all was well.

Wherever Alfredo went from that time the computer went too: over his shoulder in a carrying bag.

"This place gets worse" he said "Los fucking Angeles."

I didn't say anything.

"James Joyce was wrong. He said the Middle East was the sunken cunt of the world. He was wrong: this is the sunken cunt."

"Why don't you use that line in your play?"

"Because it's too close to what he did say! He said it in Ulysses and if you read what's written so far you'll notice that it's about him and Nora: not about his work. I'm not using any of James Joyce's lines. I don't want to get in to any of the dealing with his gobshite of a grandson."

"What do you mean?"

"I've heard they are extending copyright to seventy five years."

We stayed talking till the blood had dried on his chin.

27

When I got up the next morning I wandered into the back garden and Betty was on her knees; no she wasn't praying, although she should have been, she was weeding by the door of the cantina that I had lifted the computer from the night before. It was usually left unlocked but I had put a little match stick where a pad lock would be and it was still there.

"Patrick's leaving" she said.

"Oh well" I said.

"At least he paid his rent." she said, and carried on weeding.

I had already listened to her little tirade on my message service and it was one of the first mornings when she hadn't mentioned Alfredo's rent. Instead she had concentrated on the amount of time he let the cold water run, the fan he would leave on in the bathroom and his laundry which was going into its third week on the clothes line.

I don't think the little incident the night before had anything to do with Patrick giving notice. It was the end of the month and he had already told me of his plans to go to Beverly Hills when he asked me to go with him. I didn't say anything to Betty.

On a mid morning about a week later Betty knocked my door, opened it and put two letters on to my bed. I struggled to wake up and could just make out two letters from the bank. I guessed what they were for and as I sat up in bed to open them I heard Betty shout "Oh no!"

Then even louder "Oh no!"

I knew what it was for but I didn't think it called for a near scream.

The Schlepper's cheque had bounced which caused my rent cheque to Betty to do the same.

I put my towel robe on and went into the kitchen:

"Cheque bounced?"

"Yes" she said a little calmer than she had sounded earlier.

"Did they ask you to re-present it?"

"What do you mean?"

"Did they send the cheque back to you or did they say it was being re-presented?"

She didn't understand what I meant.

"I'll sort it out" I said "sorry."

Alfredo was sitting at his desk working when I went in. I didn't know what he was writing.

"I'm having terrible trouble" he said "I've got writer's block, I think."

He highlighted everything he had written then pressed 'delete' on the keyboard and everything disappeared from his monitor "Piece of shit" he said.

"The Schlepper's cheque bounced" I said.

"The bastard stopped payment."

"Was the treatment that bad?"

"No" he replied "it was just an excuse."

"My rent cheque has bounced too."

"I told you not to trust anybody" he said.

I didn't say anything. I just looked at him. He was very pale and hadn't bothered to shave. His cycle tee shirt was filthy which added to his unkempt appearance.

"I'm finding it hard to write anything. My typos are terrible. I keep missing the keys. Sometimes I sit a little to the right, maybe half a foot, to try and compensate, and try from over there, but it's no good. Then I keep forgetting what time of day it is, for the characters I mean, and have to keep looking back into the plot to find out if it's taking place in the day or night. I'm also forgetting the character names: which is unforgivable. It's all gone. All my writing talent has gone."

There was a pause and I listened to his room. I liked the sound of his room: there was the usual clock ticking and the sound of his floorboards creaking every time we moved "I suppose a shave is out of the question" I said.

"Feel free – have a shave!"

"Not me – you. Why don't you take a shave? It might make you feel better."

"I can't see how it could. I could never shave properly in any case. My father never taught me. Did your father teach you?"

"I don't think your father ever teaches you to shave" I said "I used to sit with him when he shaved sometimes."

"What do you mean?"

"If he's in the bathroom and we're having a chat, I go and sit on the lavatory and talk to him."

"Taking a shit?"

"No" I said "I sit on the seat. I sit on the seat and he shaves as we chat. When I was a child he would put soap on my face and pretend to shave it off. All dads do."

"My dad didn't" he said "he was always too busy."

"In business?"

I felt I might learn something about his family. He went on: "Yes. He's still the same now. Ten years ago he did a lot of work with Herzog to get the Jewish Museum built in Dublin. Do you know the Jewish Museum?"

"Yes: Walworth Road. And I know of Herzog, the Israeli President."

"Right. Born in Dublin; my father always found something to do away from his family. Even when my mother died……."

Then he stopped. "Leave it to me' he said "I'll send Milton around for the money."

"Okay" I said, and I left him to his work. Maybe he would tell me about his family some other time.

When I came in from work that evening there was an envelope on my bed: in it was seven hundred and fifty dollars in cash.

The next morning I gave Betty my rent in cash. Alfredo never mentioned it again or told me any of the details of how Milton had collected it.

28

Over the next few weeks Leah came to the house a few times. Betty was fairly polite to her and one Saturday evening Alfredo left her with me in the living room whilst he made use of the bathroom. I had managed to get them a couple of tickets for the Hollywood Bowl and she had prepared a little picnic, which she had left in the Nova parked on the drive. We were listening to a radio programme and idly chatting. She was charming in a genteel kind of way.

Harold came in and went straight to the radio and changed the station.

"There we are" he said. "The Prairie Home Companion."

So we were listening to Garrison Keillor!

"Thank you" I said.

"You're welcome. I don't expect you to understand it."

"Oh I've heard him before" I said "but I don't want to listen to him now."

I went over and re-tuned the radio. Harold didn't seem to take any notice and repeated "I don't expect you'll understand it."

Who were these fucking people I was living with? Couldn't one of them be normal? Even Harold on his visits was as nutty as Betty, Patrick and Alfredo. Maybe I was nutty too and that nutty people just attracted each other? I couldn't even wash up without one of them coming out and telling me to use more soap and make sure to rinse well. Soap? It was washing up liquid! Why couldn't they call it that? And why would they spend so much time rinsing the washing up? And why wouldn't they call it the washing up?

I would watch Patrick wash his dishes, sometimes, as I had watched my father shave, and he would run the hot water to rinse every bit of the soap from the plates as opposed to me who would leave the bubbles on the dishes for them to drop off. And look: there I go calling it soap; it's washing up liquid.

"Thank you for the tickets" said Leah.

Alfredo came in looking the same as usual: tee shirt, tracksuit bottoms and flip-flops, this time, over his socks.

"Did you ask him?"

"No" she said.

"We're doing the Rose Bowl market tomorrow" he said "Leah wants to know if you'll give us a hand to bring her stuff in here."

"What stuff?"

"The stuff we're going to sell at the market tomorrow. We don't want to leave it in the car at the Hollywood Bowl."

"Why not? It'll be quite safe" I said.

"She has to have it in here."

"What are you selling?" asked Harold.

"All sorts" said Leah "jewellery, porcelain!"

"Can I have a look?" said Harold.

"It's packed away" said Leah "you'll have to come tomorrow."

"It'll be safe at the Bowl" I said.

"We have to bring it in here or I'm not going" said Leah with a note of finality.

"Okay." I said.

As we walked to the door I called Harold and he followed. It only took about five minutes for the four of us to bring her boxes of antiques and jewellery through the front door. When we had finished Alfredo went to his room and reappeared with the laptop over his shoulder. As he did this Betty came in and stopped walking as soon as she saw the pile of boxes.

"It's okay." I said "Leah is leaving them there for the evening."

"You'll keep an eye on them for me?" said Leah. I nodded "I'm going nowhere."

"Bye." said Alfredo and he went out with Leah.

The sun was setting as they went out and she struggled with the parasol "What's that on his shoulder?" asked Betty.

"Looks like his laptop computer" I said.

It wasn't a look of surprise that came on to her face. It was more a look of confusion. She didn't take her eyes off Alfredo as he got into Leah's car.

She stood there for a moment transfixed "Let's go" she snapped at Harold and off they went.

I watched them walk down the path as I re-tuned the radio to The Prairie Home Companion.

Later in the evening Patrick knocked my door: "Do you want to come to Dan Tanna's for a last drink?"

"No thanks" I said without looking at him "I'm busy."

29

Maybe I was being unfair to Patrick, I didn't know. Sometimes his greed, selfishness, vanity and pure ignorance just got to me. He never did a favour for anybody unless there was something in it for him. He functioned like a robot not taking on board anybody else's feelings or concerns.

I could never figure out why he lent Alfredo money unless it truly was to get a role in the film he was writing; and if that was the reason he was a bigger fool than I thought.

From the time I met him to the time he came in asking me to go for a drink with him I had never seen him in need of a shave or without his contact lenses. He had a strange way of looking at you as one of his lenses was for reading and the other for distance and sometimes this gave him a lopsided cock-eyed look. It also gave his eyes a drunken look.

When I woke the next day and wandered into the living room the first thing I saw was the pile of boxes from the night before. I looked through the window to see if the Nova was in sight but it wasn't. I tap tapped on Alfredo's door.

"Come in." it sounded like a groan.

Alfredo was sitting with his head in his hands at the desk. He was groaning.

"What's the matter? Got a hangover?"

"I wish it was a hang over," he said.

"No market then?"

"I had to go to bed" he said "I didn't feel well."

"What's the matter?"

"I don't know. I keep getting electric shock-like sensations in my head and I'm dizzy."

He looked terrible.

"I keep thinking I'm going to faint. I've been awake all night."

"Sitting there?"

"Sitting here."

He got up and walked out the door.

"I have to go again."

And he disappeared into the bathroom. Too late, I thought, I had meant to use it myself but as he was in there I climbed the stairs to use that one.

Patrick's door was open and his things were gone; the broken cross-piece from the foot board was missing leaving the two side pieces standing there like goal posts without a cross-bar. So that was the end of Patrick; he got what he wanted and suffered living in the so called hovel for nine months or so and now he was off to his apartment in Beverly Hills with his monthly alimony cheque to keep him there in the manner to which he had become accustomed. It was a pity the poor sap couldn't recognize the eclectic beauty of the Silverlake craftsman's house but he couldn't. He thought he was from the upper classes and nothing could be further from the truth. The first thing he said to me when I moved in was:

"This is a Mexican area, you know. We gotta keep the place locked up."

That was the one thing that Betty didn't do: lock her house. The front door was never locked and nobody ever burgled. She said it was a safe neighbourhood and maybe she was right. Maybe the six gunshots that Alfredo heard now and again was in his imagination and maybe the police helicopter with the flashing lights and the 'Okay motherfucker drop the weapon,' that I heard now and again, was in mine. She also denied the existence of any gangs in Los Angeles and, I suppose, if she denied them, as far as she was concerned, they didn't exist.

Patrick was the opposite. He saw all Mexicans and other Latinos as gang members. He said they should all go back to Mexico not realising that they had always lived in Los Angeles - even when it belonged to Mexico as El Pueblo de Nuestra Senora la Reina de Los Angeles de Porciuncula.

I knew what ailed Alfredo; it had happened before when he had stopped taking his medicine. He came out of the bathroom, eventually, and sat at the kitchen table with me.

"Why did you stop taking your medicine?"

"How did you know I stopped?"

"Because this happened the last time you came off it. You had the shits and you were dizzy."

He didn't say anything. I went on: "Who told you to stop?"

"I don't want to be addicted to drugs." he said "I was starting to feel happy with the screenplay and helping Leah. I was starting to feel useful."

He buried his head in his hands again.

"Don't you think you'd better start taking your medicine again?"

"I don't want to" he said "I'm going to stick it out."

Then he got up and went back to the bathroom. It was Sunday. I didn't have anything to do. But we missed Patrick because he'd cancelled the Los Angeles Times and when I went up to the bathroom I noticed that he had even taken the remnants of his loo paper; mean bastard.

30

Betty would normally return to the house late on Sunday evenings. She would put her box of food into the refrigerator and go straight to bed. I never knew when she was home unless I looked inside the fridge and saw the box. The box would contain what food she had not eaten whilst out with Harold: she would eat the contents of the box for breakfast on Monday mornings no matter what it was and sometimes it would be broccoli. I don't mind broccoli but for breakfast? On Monday mornings I tried to avoid being in the kitchen at the same time as Betty because the smell of broccoli would make me want to puke.

On the Monday after Patrick left she left a message concerning the pile of boxes in the living room "I nearly fell over them when I came in," was one phrase she used.

Maybe it would have been a good idea for her to turn on some light and then she would be able to see a little better. But Betty tried to live her life on less than a dollar a week: or at least that's what it seemed like. When she went into the bathroom she would leave a little saucer over the plugholes in order to catch the drops. I wasn't sure what to do with the tiny bits of water from the saucers; she never said, so I would throw the water down the lavatory, use the wash basin and then replace the saucer.

On the day of her rant about the pile of cases, her 'left over' meal was Chinese. I don't know what it was but she had warmed it up in the microwave oven and when I got to the kitchen the smell hit me. There was broccoli in the Chinese meal and it smelled like shit.

I abandoned any thoughts of joining her; I just said good morning, went to the garden and sat on the swing.

She had disappeared when I got back and was replaced by Alfredo who looked like a bear with a sore head. He was filling Patrick's water filter bottle from the tap.

"Did he forget his bottle?"

"No" he replied "he left it for me."

31

The office where I worked was in Cahuenga Pass. They say it's a dead area, which cannot be reached by radio but I was never sure about that. The Hollywood Bowl was on the other side of the freeway from our office and was built out of the shape of the hills: a huge amphitheatre holding nearly eighteen thousand people.

The side of the pass we worked at was very rich in wild life. Outside of our office was a patio where we would sit during our breaks; one day I saw three deer through the window. One of them came within about ten feet. Two or three of us crept out, and a deer walked along a bit behind the hedge at the bottom of the hill. Then another one came and joined her. We stood there watching in silence and awe, as they were moving so close to us with their great big ears and looks on their faces like Bambi.

As we looked we heard a noise: a third deer. This one was scared so it stopped and climbed up the hill to get to the other two.

It became clear that one of them was the mother and the other two the offspring. The father, I suppose, was off in Hollywood chasing a dream. The deer came down because they were thirsty.

Two rattle snakes come down too, one day, and the gardener killed both of them by hitting them over the head with his spade and chopping their heads off. This upset one or two of the women at the office and they shouted at the gardener who didn't understand a word of English.

Even the squirrel beat up the poor snakes. The squirrel had some little ones and they would come down with their mammy and on to the patio to drink water from the sprinkler then hide and fight and play generally. One day when a snake came down somebody from the office shouted: "Come quick there's a squirrel beating up a snake."

Everybody from the office went out the back to look. It gave us smokers an excuse to light up and the rest of them just gawked.

The squirrel was knocking ten tons of shit out of the snake and we were feeling sorry for it. We could understand the squirrel, as she didn't want her young to be hurt, especially as she was a single mother with the father away, like the deer, searching for a dream and looking for a killing. Every time the snake gave up and tried to retreat up the hill the squirrel would chase it and beat it up again. The snake just couldn't win. We were really feeling sorry for it when the supervisor came out and stood there, looking at us.

We trooped back in to work. The supervisor was a beautiful black girl called Christine and I got on very well with her. Christine was around thirty years of age and was dressed in tight fitting jeans and a jean jacket.

After a few minutes the gardener came in and told us that the snake had crawled under one of the cars outside. Christine didn't take any notice.

It was a Saturday and I stayed as long as I could to try and earn some money so when the time came to close the office I was the only one left. When Christine locked the door I could see there was only one car left outside and it was Christine's; the one with the snake underneath and the snake was no longer there, according to the gardener; it had crawled up and into the engine and settled there. Christine got into her car "Usted no puede conducir eso" said the gardener.

We both looked at him.

"La serpiente del traqueteo está en el motor!"

"I think the snake's in the engine" I shouted.

I took a look underneath and, sure enough, I could see part of the snake's patterned body. We waited for the snake to come out but it didn't. We banged the car, shook it, bounced it up and down but the snake didn't move. We called Animal Rescue and they said it was nothing to do with them. 'Triple A' was next, the American Automobile Association, and they just laughed. Then Christine said she knew a cop and called him from her cellular phone. He was on duty and in the area so he was there in his patrol car within fifteen minutes or so.

They looked under the car and wouldn't believe the snake was there. I had seen it so I knew it was there and I was sure it hadn't slinked off.

It wasn't a case of being cruel or kind. If she had started the car not only would she mince the snake but the snake would ruin the engine.

When the cops came the gardener disappeared. Christine seemed to think this proved he was an 'illegal.' I thought it was a bit racist and said so. She said "What do you know about racism?"

I let it go and concentrated on the snake. One of the cops got a big stick and started poking the snake. He did quite well and the snake came down. Then it took a look at the four of us looking at it and went back up to the engine.

"It hasn't rained here for seven months," said Christine's friend, "he's just thirsty."

One of the cops suggested we walk away from the car and we stood by the car park entrance and watched the traffic for a few minutes. Christine kept her eyes on the car.

The cop was a nice guy. He told me he was from the Hollywood station on Wilcox and that his wife taught Irish dancing at a school. He gave me his number in case I was interested. When I looked later I noticed he had given me the number of the police station – just to be on the safe side, I suppose.

Christine suddenly said "There he is!"

We looked and could just see the snake disappearing into the brushwood behind where the car was parked.

"Okay" I said and started to walk down Cahuenga.

I would normally walk across a bridge, which took me to the other side of the freeway when walking down Highland passed The Hollywood Bowl but as it was Saturday and still light I figured Cahuenga wouldn't be too dangerous. It might not have been dangerous at all but it looked it and this stranger in town didn't want to take a chance.

After a few minutes Christine pulled up in her Volvo "Get in." she said.

I got in.

"Where are you going?"

"Silverlake."

"Okay" she said "I'll drop you off."

"Where do you live?"

"By the Beverly Centre" she said.

"Oh I can't drag you out of your way."

"You were the only one who stayed and cared" she said "it's the least I could do."

We drove down to Hollywood Boulevard and she signalled to turn left.

"Maybe you shouldn't turn left" I said "there's a sinkhole."

"Yes" she said "I heard about it."

So she drove straight down Cahuenga and turned left on Sunset Boulevard.

"I'm sorry I snapped at you" she said after a while.

"When?"

"When I asked you what you knew about racism."

"That's okay. I know a lot about racism. We're the niggers of Europe."

"Say what?"

"Haven't you seen The Commitments: the movie?"

"No."

"They figured they would make it as soul singers as the Irish were the niggers of Europe, Dubliners were the niggers of Ireland and Dubliners from the north side were the niggers of Dublin."

"And you're from the north side?"

I nodded.

"People say 'N' word these days."

"Sorry."

"Forget it."

We were getting on very well. I had worked at the Bowl for a few months and she was the assistant supervisor. She was a singer and sang at some of the clubs and restaurants on the west side. The job at the Bowl was a 'stop gap' for her the same as everybody else. The manager was full time but he had the attitude of a Nazi.

"Do you want a drink?" she said.

"I don't mind."

We went to the Cat and the Fiddle on Sunset Boulevard; the place where Alfredo had the meeting with the Schlepper. It was late afternoon and already the place was packed; not a seat to be had.

"Do you want to sit outside?"

"I don't mind." she said.

We found a very uncomfortable seat and the waitress came straight up to us.

"This is for food only" she said.

"How do you know we don't want food?" said Christine.

"Do you want food?" asked the waitress.

"Do you want food?" said Christine to me.

"Do you want food?" I said.

"No" she said.

"Nor me!" I said.

"Well you can't sit here." said the waitress and walked away.

"She thinks I'm your hooker." said Christine.

"No she doesn't."

"She does; betcha!"

I didn't like that; I felt embarrassed for her.

"Let's go inside." I said.

"Okay."

As we walked in I went over to the waitress.

"Why do we have to order food this time of day just to sit at that table?"

"It's our policy."

"I was just taking my boss out for a quick drink."

I felt I had to say it but the waitress didn't react either way in fact I would say she ignored me.

There were two seats available inside next to two very rough looking red-neck type men.

"Do you want to sit there – with those two gorillas?" she said.

"Why not?"

So we sat next to the two men who were, indeed, very loud; but they were friendly towards us over the course of the hour we were there. I had a couple of pints of Guinness which was okay as far as American Guinness goes. They joked that I shouldn't really be in the pub with Christine that I should be at home with her chasing her around the house.

This made us both laugh and we shook hands with them and left. They begged us to stay and wanted to buy us more drink but we had had a long enough day for a Saturday already. I didn't know if she had plans for later so I declined the drinks and we left.

"Here we are" I said when we rounded the bend to see Maltman in the distance.

We turned left and when I pointed out the house she drew up onto the drive.

It was around seven-o-clock.

"Do you want another drink?"

"What have you got?"

"Mexican Beer!"

"Sounds good."

"Okay" I said and we got out of the car.

There were no other cars around so I assumed that Betty had gone out with Harold. I wasn't sure what Alfredo was doing; his car was parked in the street, but there was no sign of life from his room. Christine sat on the porch swing and I went inside and got two bottles of beer. It didn't look as if anybody else was in the house at all as it was in darkness including Alfredo's room.

We settled down cosily on the swing and talked for a while. She was very interested in the music scene in Dublin. I knew a little bit about it and I told her of Old Mother Red Caps where they had Sunday lunchtime sessions. She seemed to know that 'The Dubliners' first started singing at a pub in Merrion Row and I told her that when I went there I was told that they had started singing somewhere else. So her information was the same as I was getting. I was a fan of The Dubliners but when they first started I was a fan of the Beatles – I told her this. She was a tremendous fan of The Beatles and wanted to know everything about them and before we knew it we had drunk three beers each and it was after nine-o-clock.

I showed her into the house and into the bathroom. The house was so quiet and I went into my room and checked to see if I had any messages. She came out of the bathroom, walked straight into my room and closed the door behind her.

"Thanks for the evening" she said and she drew a little closer to me.

I wasn't sure what was happening. I didn't want to misread the situation so I let her get close without moving. She lifted her hand to my cheek and pulled my face towards hers. Wow, this was really something. There was no tongue, or anything, but her lips were firm soft and moist like marshmallows at a campfire. We didn't get too close but things were certainly happening with my body. All my bells and whistles were working. It had been a long time since…

Tap tap: somebody was at my door. I broke away from Christine and opened it; Alfredo:

"Could I borrow some of your jam?"

"Yes, of course" I said "help yourself."

I closed the door gently behind him and smiled at Christine. She smiled back "Just as well" she said.

I walked with her to the door and saw her off. Just as well. I would have to work with her the following week and I think I remember her talking about a boy friend so just as well. Just as well that I would probably think about it for the rest of my life. It would join the other lost opportunities from my past and the many episodes of coitus-interruptus of my youth; just as well.

Alfredo came out of the kitchen "Who's the schwartzer?"

"I'm not quite sure if I like that word" I said and I went back into my room.

A few minutes later he knocked on the door again "Come in" I said.

He came in "Could I borrow some more of your jam?" Borrow!

"Help yourself" I said.

He started to close the door.

"Hang on!"

He poked his head around the door:

"What's the idea of calling her a schwartzer?"

"It's a Yiddish word....."

"I know what it is" I said interrupting him "they use it in Brooklyn and you're not from Brooklyn."

"It doesn't worry me" he said "I'm racist with everybody: micks, kikes, niggers; they're only words."

"I agree with you, Mr Lenny Bruce, but until the world grows up they're offensive."

"Can I have the jam?"

"Yes" I said "and her name is Christine."

I didn't know where he'd been all evening and I didn't really care but later in the week he mentioned Christine's singing and I had not said anything to him about it.

"How did you know she was a singer?"

"You told me" he said.

"I never said a word about it. You were listening through your window."

"Maybe I wanted to listen to some bullshit." he said "The Dubliners never played in Merrion Row. How do you know?"

"I don't."

"I saw The Dubliners when they first came out" he said "you should have asked me."

"Why would I want to ask you?" I said "We were fine as we were on the porch."

"Fine as you were" he said "you want to shit or get off the pot."

I knew what he meant by that expression; but did he want me to leave her to him or to some one else; or was he referring to a boy friend?

Another time he told me he was only listening to me as he was having trouble writing and wanted to listen to what we were talking about so he could write about Gertie. Every time I left for work he would ask me to bring home the Los Angeles Times so he could catch up with the world. I think he missed Patrick. Maybe missed having the ball thrown at him and having his glasses knocked off. He never told me if he had paid Patrick any of the money he owed. He told me to try and remember as much as I could about my bus rides and if I could hear what people were talking about. I told him he should come on the bus and listen himself.

I travelled a lot late at night: around nine-thirty or so and this would coincide with a lot of workers going home. Cleaners would get the bus from Beverly Hills and the buses would take them down town and maybe even out to the other side to East LA. Cleaners and housekeepers cleaned the rich people's houses and the rich people generally didn't bother to check if their cleaners were legal or illegal immigrants as most of them were Latino. The one thing most of the cleaners didn't have was medical insurance. So if they were ever sick they had to pay a lot of money to go to a doctor or try and find a free clinic where they would queue for hours. Most of them didn't bother and would only go to the doctor if they were really ill. This meant that they didn't have any preventative treatment and the women didn't get pap smears, breast cancer examinations or anything else but it probably meant that they had great immune systems as opposed to their rich white employers who would go to the doctor at the slightest symptom. Their rich white employers would get pills, from their doctor, which would give them anaemia, then another pill to get rid of the anaemia and a further pill to get rid of the side effects of that pill.

****

32

I came home very late one night – in the morning really at about one-o-clock and Alfredo was standing in the kitchen. He was waiting for me and had a look of anticipation on his face.

"I've been on the bus again," he said.

"I got a taxi – pity you didn't tell me."

"No" he said 'I went out to see what it was like this time of night."

"And?"

"It was fantastic" he said "I'm going again. Tonight there was a big black man sitting in front of me and he turned around and said "You got the time man?"

"Another story? I said.

He nodded; "Hang on!" I said "Let me get a drink."

There was a pot of coffee on the stove and I poured a cup.

"You ready?" he said and I sat down at the table and nodded my head.

"The black man turned around and said 'You got the time?'

'It's eleven-o-five.' I said to him.

'Hey' the black guy said 'you from London?'

'No' I said 'Dublin.'

'You been to London?"

When Alfredo said this he was looking passed me as if he was looking at the fella on the bus.

"Yes' I said 'I lived there for a while.'

'How's that Mister Fish? You know Mister Fish?'

'Does he make shirts?'

'That's the guy' he said 'he had some wonderful designs.'

'Have you been to London?'

'No I used to hang out with him in New York. Hey! You an actor?"
Alfredo liked this question. He carried on.

"No' I said."

When he said that he winked at me!

"You should be.' he said 'You sound like that guy that played Hannibal Lecter.'

'Anthony Hopkins?'

'No.'

'Oh, I know:' I said 'Brian Cox?'

'That's right' he said 'that's him.'

The woman next to me got off the bus.

'Hey! Shall I come and sit around with you – will I?'

'Yes come around' I said.

'You would do well if you were an actor. You would do well. You look like a movie star. You may be as good as Brian Cox."

Maybe Alfredo exaggerated this bit as the only actor he resembled was Charles Laughton – but I didn't say anything.

"This man was in a bad shape" he said "and it surprised me that he was fairly fluent about personalities.

'I was hit by …'

The fella went off for a bit and looked in the air."

As he said this Alfredo looked way passed me again and looked as if he was in a trance. He loved to act; he should have been an actor. As he spoke he used his emotions and gestures. His voice cracked as he said:

"I was hit by Kathleen, - what was her name? She a movie star named Kathleen. I was hit by her a couple of years ago. Ran right into me sh' did!

I'm trying man – you know what the statute of limitations..?'

'Yes' I said 'it means you must file your claim within a certain amount of time.'

'The lawyer said you just got in the door he said.'

The man looked out the window passed me then turned again:

'Are you sure you ain't no actor?'

'I'm sure."

That's what Alfredo said to him but he should have said yes. He went on:

'Hey man. Keep in touch. I try to be good. I try to keep quiet and mind my business. I went up to Chicago, man – I robbed the bank. My mother was dying and I robbed the bank. I went right in there and cos I was so big they gave me the money. I had to do three years, man. I try to keep quiet now."

As Alfredo said this he really acted the role.

'Times are hard' I said.

'You want some money, man? Here I give you some. Here!'

He reached into his pocket.

'No no no no' I said.

'I'm staying at the Panama Hotel: room one-one-eight. You come and see me. We go and get sumpen t'eat; we can talk.'

'Yes we must.'

The bus travelled a while and we were in silence.

'Shall I go see my lawyer?'

'Wouldn't hurt to remind him about you.'

'Might sort my life out if I get some money from Kathleen. She a bitch - she dint even check to see if I got to the hospital. I had to teach myself to walk again.'

'Did she break your leg?' I said.

'Yeh, my tibia – you know the tibia?'

I looked down and his knee reached the seat in front. I pointed 'Yes! That bone there!'

'You're right man. You know.'

I could see that the bus was nearing my stop here.

'Got to get off' I told him.

'Okay then, man.'

We shook hands as we got up and I moved passed him.

'Panama Hotel, room one-one-eight' he said.

'Okay.'

I knew there wouldn't be much of a chance of meeting up with him. It was just impracticable. In any case I already had a shiralee at home with you.

I walked to the bus door. He called out 'Hey man: room one-one-eight. My name's Mitchell!'

I shouted back Alfredo Hunter.

'Okay Alfredo Hunter' he said.

'Room one-one-eight.' I repeated and I got off the bus.

I walked to the traffic light ready to cross Sunset Boulevard and waited for the lights to change. As I waited the bus came passed and Mitchell waved. I waved back and walked up the hill to the house and here I am now."

"I never see any of this on any bus" I said.

"You never look!"

He went to the fridge, grabbed his ice cream and spoon and walked into the garden.

I poured another cup of coffee lit a cigarette and joined him in his usual place: standing on the deck at the guesthouse looking at the stars and eating ice cream from a gallon carton. There was a slight chill in the air, as October had arrived and it got that way then, so I was surprised that he was just wearing a tee shirt.

"What are you looking for?"

"Nothing," he said "maybe inspiration. When I look up there I see nothing but the moon and the stars in the heavens. I can still hear, of course, and I can imagine what's going on around me but it doesn't take too much to cut it all out. Then I see the stars and I am alone; alone with thoughts of what I am going to do next; maybe a little plot line or a piece of dialogue; maybe to forget it all and top myself.

I can stare at the wall inside my room but the décor would drive me mad even with the light out, but out here I can feel the stars. I can feel them …

Did somebody ever say that they could feel the stars 'shitting the light down on them?' That's a grand expression even if nobody said it. Sometimes when I look at the stars, like on the night of the Bloomsday Blackout, I think of what I had been doing previously: the girl showing us her drawers on the stage whilst she read her lines popped straight into my head and I knew I could write a story about her."

Then suddenly he said "Your boy friend was here today."

"Who?"

"Patrick! He asked about you."

There was a certain innuendo in his voice.

"He's not that way inclined" I said "he has grandchildren."

"Doesn't matter a God damn; people have turned gay at all ages and marital status. I had a fella after me once."

I laughed.

"Don't laugh. I was adored once, you know."

He hadn't shaved again and looked filthy and slovenly.

"Bit of Shakespeare that."

He had his hands in his pockets and he turned around to face me.

"I'm going into a hole" he said, "and there's nothing I can do about it."

"What do you mean?"

"I'm going into a bout of depression. Did you know depression is a potentially fatal disease? Most of us who have it commit suicide. Without knowing about it you have stopped me a few times; I don't know why!"

"Maybe because I'm stupid."

"Could be," he said in all seriousness. "You're just a thick Mick, really and life is simple and Catholic and straightforward. It must be wonderful to be ignorant."

He had a good nature so I knew he wasn't trying to hurt me.

"Maybe I just love you." he said.

"Now who's on the turn?" I joked.

"Not that way; you're like a brother."

He took two spoonfuls of ice cream.

"What did Patrick want?"

"What do you think?" he chuckled.

"Money?"

"Yes," he said, "or your arse."

We both laughed at that. I knew that it wouldn't make any difference what I said. He would go into his hole. He would spend vast amounts of time alone in his room looking at his lap top computer, as if he was waiting for a message from it, and listening to the Jewish music he was so fond of; if he turned the music off he would have the company of the ticking and the squeaking of the floorboards. His long walks with the dog in Dog Shit Canyon might take him out of his depression temporarily or give him ideas as to how he could kill himself but as he had a great affection for the dog he wouldn't kill himself and abandon the dog in the park. So he would go back to his room and be a slob and watch the worst programmes on television whilst stuffing himself with ice cream to wait for the other side of the hole.

"When did I stop you?"

"I suppose I was all set to do it and I thought about you; thought about how hopeless you are and how lost you always look in this foreign land: dressed as if you are taking the DART across Dublin on a cold winter's day. Look at you! Do you know if you travelled the United States and arrived at some small town dressed like that someone would come along and beat you up?"

"Someone would come along?" I said.

"That's what I said. Someone would come up to you in a bar or a restaurant and just beat the shite out of you. You should get yourself some jeans."

"Maybe I should dress like you? Like a hippy!"

We both laughed.

"Are you still off the medicine?"

"Yes, he said, I'm going to start taking St Johns Wort."

"Where did you get that idea?"

"I read a lot," he said "if I get out the other side of this hole, IF - - I'll start taking it. Or I may go back on the medication."

"Might be a good idea to go on the medicine."

"Thank you doctor." he said.

"Fuck you." I said.

"I was sitting in the cantina the other night" he said "the night you came back with Christine and I didn't mean to spy. I was sitting in the dark just smelling history in there and I couldn't help hearing you. If I had moved about, I would have disturbed you. If I had let you know I was there by coughing or something like that I would have disturbed you that way too. I was trapped in there. I'm sorry."

"Why did you ask for the jam?"

"I don't know. I just fancied some jam."

I wasn't sure whether to buy that one. I changed the subject:

"So when were you adored?"

"I've been adored all my life." he said "I was better looking than you. It was in Tunisia."

"Tunisia?"

"Yes: a Jew in Tunisia; could be the title of a book."

"When was this?"

"Only a couple of years ago: January ninety-three. I was living in San Francisco at the time my mother died in Dublin. She died and I couldn't make it back in time for the funeral. I had no money. By the time I got the money together she was buried; we're quick at burying our own us Jews."

"Was it sudden?"

"Not really. She was old and it had to happen sometime, I suppose. I was full of guilt when I got home and nobody made me feel any better so I fucked off."

"To Tunisia?"

"Yes."

"Why didn't you come straight back here?"

"I had to hang around for legal reasons in case the will was contested. So I went to a travel agent and asked for the first flight out of Dublin – first package deal; somewhere not too far."

"And you got Tunisia?"

"Yes. But I enjoyed it. I liked the idea that I was a Jew and they didn't know it. My white hair is not exactly Jewish and I don't have a particularly Jewish name. Some of them thought I was an Arab, as I have this sallow kind of complexion, and I'm sure some of them guessed I was Jewish, but I thought it would have been ironic if I was gay and let an Arab arse bandit fuck me.

The weather was glorious after the few miserable days in Dublin with the fucking rain. I would walk the beaches some days in the sun and the Arab boys would ride their horses down the beach at full pelt. I still have this vision of a horse belting along the beach with an Arab boy on its back holding on for dear life and yet, at the same time, under complete control; as he passed me I had to squeeze my eyes to see through the powerful sun and as the back of his shirt, inflated by the speed of the horse, ballooned out behind him, it looked like a mirage. Maybe I could even see smiles of delight on the faces of both horse and man as they became one. I was sorry at the time that I didn't have some sort of movie camera to capture it; but I'm not a cameraman, I'm a writer, and I captured it up here forever. One day my pen will manifest it back to life. The fella with the pen has the power of life and death over his characters so if one of my characters is depressed I can put him out of his misery and get him to take his own life. I can make him do it as painlessly as possible so he can slink off into the after life in peace. I don't have to give a reason: I can make the Arab boy decide that life will never get any better than riding that horse along that beach at that particular moment and I can get him to throw himself off for no better reason than that he wants to choose where and when to die. I wish someone could put me out of my misery."

He liked telling stories. It gave him vigour and he sat down on the top step of the deck and took a mouth full of ice cream.

"Were you attracted to him?"

"I was attracted to the horse."

He laughed.

"I went to a place called Hammamet and one day I was walking down a street and an Arab shopkeeper wanted to swap pens with me. I had asked him where I could get some good couscous and, after we swapped pens, he said 'take my sister with you' but I didn't. I bought some coffee in an out door café instead."

"The next day I went to the same café and the waiter treated me like a long lost brother. He didn't hug me, or anything, but patted me on the shoulder a few times. That time I had a couple of cups of coffee and a fruit filled pancake. From there I went for a wander and found a bench to sit on and saw some kind of official government car. It was parked in the street and was blocking traffic. The people stood back and looked on in awe at this wondrous sight. Can you imagine it: a big posh car standing there so superior with people looking at it as if it was some kind of coronation coach waiting for a queen? I looked around and saw an Arabic fella looking at me: he was very well dressed with his Gucci watch, French jeans and a very smart pair of cowboy boots with metal toecaps; it was the boots that drew my attention to him but when I looked up to his face he was looking at me: I looked away immediately. The car was there for some time and I waited on the bench wondering what the government official would look like when he appeared. The fella with the boots didn't move from the spot. Maybe he was wondering about the government official too or maybe he was going to assassinate him but he kept looking at me and I started to feel uneasy. It crossed my mind that he was an Arab and I was a Jew and maybe he wanted to expose me or maybe he had, in fact, taken a fancy to me. Men tend to stick together in Tunisia till they meet a woman to marry. They hang around in coffee shops drinking coffee till all hours. They sit outside and inside these coffee shops – not like the one I was at eating the pancake – but huge dark places and they talk and play board games.

So I was sitting on this bench waiting to see if I'm going to see a celebrity coming out. I'm waiting with the rest of the people in Hammamet and the poor people are passing in front of me looking towards the big car with the flags on it.

There was a fella walking who had no feet. He had some Wellington boots on and I could see they were folding over making it impossible for feet to be in there. I looked at him as he walked passed and he walked passed the fella with the Gucci watch and the French jeans who was still looking at me.

All this time Gucci had his hands behind his back and, as the fella with no feet went passed him, I noticed he had put the Fedora, he had been holding, onto his head and he posed for a few minutes. I either got bored with waiting for the celebrity or got cold feet so I upped and went to a small market, close by, to buy a bottle of water. When I looked up, after I picked up the bottle from the shelf, I saw the Fedora behind one of the lines. He was buying water too. I could see him closer and he was around twenty-five or so and looked very rich. I let him get served first as I walked off to look for something else.

Now I might have been imagining all this or it might all have been a coincidence. He might have been setting me up to get beaten by his friends or might not have noticed me at all but when I came out of the supermarket I couldn't see him so I had another wander and found a big place called the Medina which looked like a castle from the outside. Inside it was full of shops: it was like an antique centre but with thousands of trinkets, shoes and leather bags – you name it.

After a few minutes of window-shopping I saw the Fedora again. He was looking at me from across an aisle. Now that wasn't my imagination.

Then I heard 'hello!' I looked around and there were two girls sitting outside one of the shops. It was the 'pen swapper's' sister from the day before and her friend.

'Hello' I said.

One of the girls grabbed my arm and gently led me into the shop to look around. I had a look and everything in there had been recently mass-produced. Models of Arabs on camels, little saddles – you know the kind? Actually there was quite a good chess set I thought about but there was nothing in there for me, not really, so I turned to go out. The pen swapper's sister blocked my path to get out. She was very beautiful, maybe about eighteen years old; you know how beautiful some of the Arab girls can be? She wouldn't move from the spot and when I tried to go around her she stood closer to me and looked at me with those, those – they must have been almost violet eyes! I'm not joking but I'm sure I felt my sphincter go and I felt so weak. She could have done anything she liked to me and I half expected a hand on my dick any moment but she suddenly let me pass. She must have seen some kind of panic in my eyes. So any doubts about my sexuality I had in the episode earlier had disappeared."

"Did you have any doubts?"

"Not really."

"Not really?"

"No. I think I might have been flattered: a man of my age with a younger man following me."

"What age?"

"Ah ha!" he said.

He wouldn't tell me his age.

"Might have been after your money?"

"No. He was rich. I was adored once: when I came out of the Medina the Fedora was still waiting but I got a cab and went back to my hotel."

So I learned a little bit about Alfredo that night.

33

A couple of days later, on Sunday morning, I woke to find that the boxes of antiques had disappeared from beside the front door. So they had finally gone to the market. That is unless some one had crept in through the usually unlocked door over night and made it away with Leah's gear.

It was good to have the house to myself for a change. I could put the radio on in my room and leave the doors open whilst I wandered from room to room. I thought about taking a walk to the cinema on Sunset Boulevard but decided that the opportunity to be alone at home for no other reason than it didn't arise often was too good to miss. I knew that Alfredo and Leah would be back as soon as they finished at the market and Betty would be in too eventually.

She arrived at around three in the afternoon. I decided to use the radio in the front room, by the door, to listen to the afternoon programmes on Public Radio. I fancied, somehow, sitting on the swing in the front porch listening to it whilst writing some letters home. I worried about my pregnant sister in Dublin as her feet had begun to swell and my mother had told me she was getting so excited about the expected birth. I hoped that my mother would not interfere too much and leave her alone to take care of things with her husband. It seems as though my mother was staying away from her though for some reason and my sister spent a lot of time around at my mother's. Maybe she felt more comfort there than at her own place where she would be expected to get on with the chores.

I had my writing implements ready and was just getting a beer from the fridge when I heard the radio being switched off. I walked into the living room and it was Harold. There was something he wanted to catch on television so my peaceful day was at an end.

"Hi." he said without looking up.

Betty came through the front door and did a kind of double take when she saw that the pile of packed bric-a-brac had been removed from its usual place. I went back into my room to write home and drink my beer. It was their house but I always got that feeling, whenever I was a guest, of resenting the hosts when they disturbed me. I stopped watching television at Betty's, as she was probably the worst host I had ever experienced. When I first moved in with her and Patrick I would be watching television and on more than one occasion, if I had gone to the bathroom, I would come back to find the room in darkness and the television switched off. It was as if I didn't exist.

34

Leah and Alfredo had a good day at the market. She gave him enough money to make him feel useful and he had bought a few large cartons of ice cream to make him feel better.

He was a different person for a few days. It was as if he was a child playing at being a grown up with a job. He didn't really care how much she gave him; he had risen early and gone out to earn a crust. Something he didn't seem used to.

We talked about his experience a few times during the week and he told me he had tried to get Leah to lay the stall out differently so that the customers could see the various pieces for sale.

He said "She keeps hiding the good stuff at the back."

But it was good that he was conscientious about the stall; it showed he cared.

"Have you started taking the *St John's Wort* yet?" I asked.

"I'm still taking my medication." He said "I haven't come out of the hole yet. I have a definite offer for my play."

"When?"

"End of January."

"That gives you over three months to finish it off."

"Yes we've got work to do."

"There goes that old word 'we' again." I said.

He smiled.

"What ever happened to good old medicine?"

"What?"

"When did medicine go out and medication come in?"

I shrugged.

He shrugged; "I've been living here too long."

35

Betty asked me to go to Equity, actors' union, and to SAG, the screen actors union, and put some notices up to say she had a room to rent: it didn't cost anything to advertise. I drove down to the two offices in Betty's other car, which was an old Dodge Dart. It was a great thrill for me to drive, as I loved old American cars. I went the long way to Wilshire Boulevard for SAG and went as far west as Doheny to make the drive back along Sunset Boulevard longer. I was Mister America Graffiti enjoying the change from travelling on the bus.

Patrick had asked her time and again if he could drive it but she wouldn't let him; I don't know why she let me but she did.

On my journey to work I had the choice of three buses to catch at the bottom of Maltman Avenue on Sunset Boulevard.

That was the extent of my knowledge of Los Angeles. I had been to the beach a few times at Santa Monica and Venice and I'd been to the Farmer's

Market on Fairfax Avenue. I knew of Beverly Hills, the Hollywood Hills, Pacific Palisades and other names from the lists of telephone numbers I was given at work but they meant very little to me. So the ride in the Dodge Dart was a real treat I felt free and, somehow wild and unsupervised; a bit like a prisoner out after a long stretch.

Something Betty had said about Alfredo in her morning call disturbed me a little: she said she thought Alfredo was receiving money in the mail; she didn't say where from but the fact that she was noticing mail gave me the idea that I would like a post office box; they were very cheap so I went to a post office in Cherokee Avenue and signed up.

36

For a few days Alfredo tended to stay in his room. I guessed it was something to do with his illness and I expected to see him when he came out of the hole he had mentioned. He would come in to the kitchen whilst I was brewing coffee and stand with his back to the cooker. Sometimes he would slide down the fridge and sit on the floor in front of it resting his back against the door. When I asked him how he was he would always reply and would always smile. But the smile wasn't the usual warm Alfredo smile. There was something about his eyes: something that said 'I'm in pain.' It was as if he had spent the night crying in his sleep and couldn't quite get the last tear to drain away.

I would usually get on with what I was doing and tried to leave him to his own counsel. It wasn't the time to suggest he commit suicide as he might take me seriously.

After about ten days of this, as he was sitting on the floor he said: "Funny thing, the brain, isn't it?"

He said this and then got up from the floor, grabbed his pot of oatmeal, with the million and one herbs in, and went out. I knew he couldn't say something like that and leave it without coming back to finish the thought so I waited.

Sure enough, when he had finished his breakfast he came back and sat at the table with me.

"It's a funny, horrible, frightening and beautiful thing. It makes .... it gives me this lust for knowledge and love of music but then .... then it sends me reeling into a black hole and sometimes I wonder if I'm ever going to get out!"

He hadn't been out since he had returned from the Rose Bowl flea market and looked very pale sitting there at the table.

"I should be feeling wonderful. I had a great day on Sunday with Leah and she wants me to help her every month but....."

He had his hands together as if he was praying and he folded his fingers over to make a double fist squeezing so tight that I was sure he was hurting himself. I put my hand on top of his and gently opened his hands.

"..... I can't," he said. "I can't go with her for the moment. I don't want to go out anywhere."

"I'm sure she'll understand" I said.

"Not important whether she understands or not; it's me. I want to go but I can't. Can you answer the question?"

"I don't think so." I said.

"Why does my beautiful brain torture me so? Why?"

"I'm just a thick Mick" I said "I don't know."

"Hippocrates was right" he said "only from the brain spring our pleasures and happiness – but the same organ makes us mad!"

"Is that what he said?"

"Words to that effect."

He lifted his head up and looked, desperately, into my eyes.

"If I committed suicide on Stinson Beach would you come to my funeral?"

The question came from nowhere: it stunned me. It was as if he had been meaning to say this to me for some time and had chosen this moment.

"Do you mean just me or your family too?"

"My family won't be here for my funeral. I wasn't there for my mother. We are Jews – we can't wait."

"Does the Jewish faith recognize suicide?"

"Nobody recognizes suicide" he said "just a manic-depressive."

With that he got up slowly and went out. I didn't know what to do. I didn't know any of his friends and the only person I knew that knew him, apart from Betty, was the Schlepper. I had heard of Milton but he had only been to the house when I was out and I didn't know his telephone number.

As I was leaving for work sometime later I tapped on his door. There was no reply but I opened his door in any case. He was sitting at his desk writing.

"What are you writing?" I said.

"Porn!"

"What?"

"Porn" he repeated. "How do you think I live? I don't have some rich benefactor sending me money. I write scripts for porn movies."

"No wonder you're depressed" I said "you should be finishing off your James Joyce play."

"I have to live" he said "I can't even pay my rent but I have to eat. I know Betty calls you and complains about me.   She calls you from the garden and I hear her."

"How long have you known?"

"Forever," he said. "She wakes me every morning with her telephone call to the congressman and then goes into the garden to call you. I'm usually in the bathroom and can hear every word. I don't bother to listen any more. I'll get the rent to her someday. I didn't do it intentionally – it just happened.

It's always been the same – all my life. I've always been broke. I always have such good intentions with my planning and I always run out of money. I remember once I needed some money and I called my sister at work in Dublin. I needed two pounds; just two pounds. She couldn't get to me but she told me to come to the car park where she worked and she would leave the two pounds under the passenger seat of her car; she left her car open for me. I ran into somebody I knew just as I got to the car – one of the writers from Bewley's – and he said 'Ah! Shag it! It happens to us all. Since then I haven't worried. It's all up here."

He tapped his forehead.

"That's where we're rich."

"Okay" I said "I'll see you later."

"It's about ten weeks before they want the play for the public reading. We've got plenty of time."

"There goes that word 'we' again."

37

Slowly, but surely, over the next few weeks Alfredo started to get better, little bit at first; he started to come out of his room if he heard me go into the kitchen. Then he started knocking my door and saying: "Buy you a cup of coffee?"

We would go to the kitchen whilst he drank water from Patrick's bottle and I drank black coffee. He told me that he had taken Milton with him to collect my seven hundred and fifty dollars from the Schlepper but the Schlepper would not give him any of it unless he promised to write a pornographic film script. They had haggled and argued for a time as Alfredo wanted payment up front and finally settled on two scripts for eight hundred. That was when he had put my money on the bed. He said the first porn script was easy enough to write but he was struggling with the second one. I told him not to use the royal 'we' when writing porn.

I came home one Saturday evening from the movies and as I approached the house I could see the dog from next door at the fence. He was looking over to the back of our garden, which meant that Alfredo was there so I went round the back to look. Sure enough, there he was: sitting on the sun deck looking up to the stars. "What are you looking for?" I said "A shower of meteors?"

"I've just had my shower of meteors. A shower of meteors is a bad omen to the Indians" he said.

"But you're not an Indian."

"I know. But I am one of the indigenous people. I always compare myself to the Indian."

I sat next to him on the deck.

"Welcome back."

"Thank you." he said.

"How's the porn?"

He laughed "Finished."

"Answer me a question: what do you know about the stars?"

"Not a fecking thing." he said "I just like to look. If I start to learn about the Great Bear, or Cassiopeia or anything like that my inspiration will go and I'll start to write about stars and planets and not the inspiration looking at them gives me."

"I'll have to go." I said and walked towards the house.

Before he had gone outside, Alfredo had been filling Patrick's jug with water from the tap. Before doing this he had washed his bowl that he had eaten pasta from, and left the pasta to block the sink. So when I got into the kitchen the water was running into the bottle, overflowing that and overflowing the sink and onto the kitchen floor. I turned the water off straight away. When I looked closely it was easily one inch deep and, obviously, flooding the cantina below.

I shouted "Alfredo!"

"What?"

"Alfredo!"

"What?"

"Just come here." I said.

He came into the house and I showed him the mess. He stood there mystified. I located the mop and started to mop the water up. It took a long time. When we had finished he said "I'll tell Betty I mopped the floor."

I didn't take any notice of his mumbling. We found some newspaper and dried it with that. When it was as good as I could get it he went back to his room. As he left me he repeated "I'll tell Betty I gave it a really good mopping."

The next morning the message on the machine from Betty said that the cantina was flooded and it hadn't rained.

I went into Alfredo and he was writing "Shall I tell her you mopped it good and proper?"

"Yes" he said "tell her I gave it a really good mopping."

"And the cantina?"

He looked up "What?"

There was water all over the bench in the cantina, in every tin that held the old nails, in the socket sets, on all the wooden beams and there was still a one-inch reservoir on the floor. I took all the tools out and dried them in the sun and tried to dry the beams as much as I could with an old cloth. I put the old bags of cement into the bin as they were soaking wet; then I mopped the floor. The cantina would never be the same again. It would never smell the same and all the oldness and character had gone.

After a while Alfredo came out to look but instead of coming to look at the cantina he went to the cellar, which was under my room. Then he came back round "How the fuck could the water get there?" he said.

I didn't answer him and he went back to his room. I had spent a lot of time trying to convince him that he was not a failure and not a loser so I didn't know how this would affect him. I went to his room and he didn't seem too bothered: 'Not a bother on him' as my mother would say.

He was still at the writing desk and said: "I was only thinking the other day; I might ask Betty if I can stay on here as a sort of caretaker. To look after the property: don't suppose there's much chance of that now?"

I looked at him to see if he was serious.

"I'm sorry about the cantina" he said "it was my favourite room in the house. It reminded me of when I was a little boy in Dublin. The next door neighbour built a shed at the bottom of his garden. He would go there on Saturday afternoons and listen to the football match on his radio. I thought it was great. I could hear it from our garden and I would sit by the fence every Saturday afternoon in the football season. He was an Aston Villa fan and he would cheer if they scored a goal. I got to know a lot about English football from his radio. One day, when they were all out, I sneaked into his shed. It was getting dark but I could see his tools and boxes just like the cantina. I never heard him ever using the tools. He just went in there for peace and quiet, I think. Anyway, this day when I sneaked in, I looked around for the radio and as I looked I saw him asleep in an armchair. Fast asleep he was in the shed. At first I thought he was dead and I just froze to the spot; I couldn't move. I hadn't woken him up when going in and, logically, I shouldn't wake him going out but that never occurred to me. I just stood there and then he snored or made some kind of noise; frightened the shite out of me it did; so I walked backwards towards the door, my eyes fixed on him in case he woke up; then I made a very slight noise, trod on something I think, and he moved. I stopped; frightened to breathe."

He was silent for a few moments. Not moving. Not looking directly at me but looking just passed me towards the door.

"What happened then?"

"Can't remember." he said.

"See you later" I said and I went out.

38

Betty was very upset about the mess to the cantina; it took precedence over every other subject in the daily voice mail. It had been a dear place to sit when it was dry and it had probably been in that condition for fifty years. Some of the nail boxes were that old and the smell and feel of the place had disappeared completely since the flood. Everybody was upset, not just Betty, but I think the person most upset was Alfredo. He had started to sit in the room to think during the daylight hours when he couldn't see the stars; he loved the dark and the smell and the privacy. He tried it a few times after the flood but would leave after a few minutes.

I tried to put things out in the November sunshine, which was a lot cooler than the August sunshine but was, nonetheless, sunshine. Alfredo would see what I was trying to do and would say 'why don't you just forget it.' Sometimes he would say it with a certain amount of despair in his voice and once or twice I wondered why he just wouldn't come and give me a hand. Maybe it was just as well that he took to hiding in his room, as there was nothing he could have done. I was trying to make Betty think all was not lost.

Communications between Betty and Alfredo were non-existent and both of them spoke to each other through me. But I would not pass messages on. Betty would leave all she had to say on my machine and Alfredo would listen to her recording the message live from the bathroom, if she was calling from the garden, and ignore it. Alfredo would say things he wanted me to pass on to Betty but I never did. One thing Alfredo wanted was Patrick's old room. I thought he was unreasonable expecting Betty to give him another room when he didn't pay for the first one and I told him so. Another thing he complained about was the lack of some of the prime cable television channels. Again I told him I thought he had a lot of chutzpah if he was serious.

Betty had decided to move to the guest house on top of the garage as it had been completed. She said she would be able to rent the two rooms upstairs – Patrick's old room and the one she used – if she got any response from the notices I had put up at SAG.

She seemed very comfortable in the guest house and probably felt safer away from Alfredo although he would never have done any harm to her.

One day she asked me if I would like to go to Las Vegas for thanksgiving to visit her daughter. I decided against it and she went with Harold instead.

Alfredo said he would take me out to thanksgiving lunch.

Thanksgiving didn't mean anything to me. I had heard about it, of course, but didn't realize that it was such a big holiday in America: turkey day they call it.

When the big day arrived Alfredo told me to be ready at twelve-thirty, as our table had been booked for one-o-clock. I wasn't sure how to dress so decided to go casual. I needn't have worried about it as Alfredo wore his usual tracksuit and flip-flops.

He took me to the world famous Laugh Factory on Sunset Boulevard.

When we drove up I could see the sign, which said that there was a free thanksgiving dinner to all actors, comedians and writers. I had wondered what the snag was and it became clear.

"I'm not an actor or performer." I said.

"Don't worry about it!"

We had to queue outside and a lot of the others waiting in the queue were kind of homeless looking; that was the whole idea. The meal was delicious: turkey with all the trimmings. The meals were dished up by television celebrities, which didn't mean much to me as I very rarely watched television. In fact since I had moved in to Betty's I had watched the television when the Israeli Prime Minister, Rabin, was assassinated, when the Beatles Anthology was shown and FA Cup Final between Everton and Manchester United: which I would have enjoyed had it not been for the constant interruptions from Betty who walked in and out of the living room every ten minutes or so laughing at the top of her voice at me watching television at seven in the morning.

The comedians who performed that day performed mainly to an audience of down and outs. I felt embarrassed but I laughed at the performers jokes – if they were funny. Sometimes they weren't funny and one comedian who was about as funny as toothache shouted, "Laugh! It's free" a few times when the audience found their turkey dinners more entertaining than his act.

Alfredo ignored the whole proceedings and didn't even eat.

I thanked him on the way back and he took a CD from his belt and put it into a portable CD player, which he then plugged into the hi-fi system of his car. I joked that this doubled the price of his car and he actually laughed.

The CD he played was of Canadian gypsy type of music: almost Cajun and when one of the tracks came on he started to cry. Every time the song finished he would start it again. The tears were rolling down his face. By the time we reached home he was a blubbering mess.

"What was that about?" I asked as we got indoors.

He didn't say anything so I left him to his misery as he seemed to be enjoying it and went back to my room. An hour or so later he was in the back garden dumping his laundry over the clothesline. When he had dumped the last garment Betty and Harold came back from Las Vegas and as she climbed the steps to her room, with Harold trotting along behind her carrying a few bags, they both looked at Alfredo's laundry in disgust; neither of them saying a word.

She had returned rather early, I thought, but then I remembered she was preparing some kind of party for the Sunday afternoon. After a few minutes Harold emerged from the guest house carrying two plastic shopping bags and I heard him dumping the contents of them into the refrigerators. I just sat looking through my window; I didn't want to go and say hello. I couldn't get over the fact that it was November and still very warm. Then I heard Alfredo coming out of his room, go to the kitchen and open one of the fridges. He must have guessed that Harold had left some goodies for Betty. I didn't hear the fridge door close, so can only assume he was still ogling at the goodies. Then I saw Betty come out and start to walk towards the house - maybe to raid the fridge too? When she was half way across the lawn I heard the fridge door close and Alfredo go back to his room and close his door. There was silence in his room. He didn't play any music or put his television on so I could clearly hear Betty open one of the fridges then she opened the other one. I knew what the subject of her telephone message next morning would be. As I sat back on my chair I was sure I could smell human shit.

****

39

I could still smell the shit around the downstairs of the house for the next few days. Nobody else mentioned it so I put it to the back of my mind.

Sunday came and at around three-o-clock Betty had her garden party. It had been three days since Alfredo had done his laundry so it was still on the clothesline when the first guests arrived; apart from dumping the clothes over the line without pegs, he, as usual, hadn't separated his washing into whites and coloureds, in the washing machine; everything went on a very hot wash then he had hung the laundry over the line in a sort of long multi coloured hanging snot. Also at the same time the guests arrived he had decided to go to his room and put some music on very loudly: the same music that made him cry on Thanksgiving Day.

Betty sent Harold to knock on Alfredo's door but the music was so loud that Alfredo could not hear him shouting: "Guests arriving! Put music down!"

"Tell him to get his laundry off the line too!" screamed Betty.

After she screamed I saw her go into the garden to greet her guests in a gentler manner from the one I had heard. Everybody was walking around carrying plates and drinks and smiling and drinking. Betty was going from one to the other like some demented gorgon and Harold returned and proceeded to follow her closely. When he got too close to her she turned quickly and whispered something into his ear. It wasn't hard to guess what she had said as he made for the house and Alfredo's door again. As before Alfredo ignored Harold's shouting and knocking.

I had been invited to the party but had decided not to go. Besides it was more fun to watch them from my window.

There was one woman with rather nice red hair pushed up to reveal an attractive neck and she must have been quite tasty in her day. When somebody took her photograph she brushed, what looked like, a tear from under her eye then she took a walk to the swing and posed for more shots. When the photographer had finished taking photographs, the red head put on a pair of sunglasses, with red ribbons attached, and sat on the swing alone. A few minutes later a man came and sat next to her.

The dog was looking through the fence at the entire proceedings wondering if anybody would send over a piece of food. But the only person in the building that would do such a thing was sitting in his room playing music very loudly.

A young blonde girl arrived with her boyfriend and everybody started throwing their arms around them; the dog, watching this, climbed onto its two rear legs, wagging its tail, hoping for a stroke but, as with the food, the only person that would do such a thing was sitting in his room playing music very loudly. And all the time the smell of a sewer permeated the air making each of them think that somebody at the party was dropping smelly messages.

The man sitting on the swing next to the red head lit his pipe causing the red head to get up and sit somewhere else. When she did this the young blonde sat next to the pipe smoker and lit a cigarette.

Apart from the blonde and her boyfriend everybody at the party was closer to sixty than fifty and some of them even older. They looked as if they were visiting from some local old actor's home.

A little old lady appeared on the steps of the guesthouse: she was blonde and wearing a purple trouser suit and as she hovered around the deck, close to the door, admiring the roses, she looked like a purple haze.

As I looked at them I noticed my room smelling as if somebody had dumped some baby's nappies in a corner so I went to the bathroom to see if I could find anything wrong. I could still smell it in there but not so strong so I knocked on Alfredo's door. He couldn't hear me knock so I went in.

He was sitting at his desk typing and crying.

"Can you smell that shit?" I said.

"Maybe you're standing too close to yourself," was his reply.

I didn't take any notice of his humour.

"Are you going to get your washing off the line and put your music down?"

"Why should I?"

"It's like Christmas to them," I said "can't you have the decency to give them a bit of peace?"

"Christmas?" he said, "You know my religion."

"Yes," I said "Pagan."

Very quietly he said, "You're right."

When I went back to my room I could see them in the garden sitting around looking at each other in the twilight.

Then I heard the music in Alfredo's room go off followed by the great man himself taking his laundry off the line. He didn't speak or look at any of the guests and they, in turn, ignored him. As he walked back to the house he took a slight detour and said hello to the dog.

After he left, the guests at the party started taking group photographs; one of them picked up an empty bottle of wine and pretended it was a trumpet – others did playful things too and as I settled down to read my book I heard Alfredo going out.

Every time the music played it reminded Alfredo of a girl he used to know in England. He said she looked like a very beautiful Indian – an American Indian. The only difference is that she had very long black curly hair: 'it went right down to her arse" was how he put it.

They lived together in various parts of England working as stage managers in the theatre. This was a side to Alfredo that I didn't know. The girl figured she was the reincarnation of a Lakota princess.

I didn't know that Alfredo had been a stage manager and he told me that that was where he learned his art. He would never use the word craft always art.

When I sat with him on the deck outside the guest house he would look up and explain at great length the difference between art and craft. He loved cricket and would call the bowlers artists because they had mastered the art of bowling.

"You can always tell people that treat everything like a craft" he would say "because what they do isn't art.'

I think half the time he was quoting Oscar Wilde.

He worked, with his girl friend, at the theatres in Northampton, Cheltenham and Birmingham. When he said 'Birmingham' he said "….and of course Birmingham."

Obviously something happened in Birmingham but he didn't tell me straight away.

He met her in Northampton. He was a twenty-five year old just across on the boat from Ireland and not long out of university and she attended the high school there. The theatre was very close to the high school and he met her as she was a fan of the theatre.

I tried to get a flavour of the times from him so I could try and work out his age but he was very crafty.

He noticed the girl because of her beauty and one day he saw her parking a motor cycle in the street. He didn't know who it was until he saw her take the crash helmet off and he said he fell in love with her as he saw her black curls cascade down her back.

"Gonna take me for a ride?" he said

The girl put the crash helmet back on and said "Hop on."

"What about your crash helmet?" I said.

"We didn't have to wear them in those days."

He eventually got her a job at the theatre as a kind of intern – although they didn't call them interns in those days. She was eighteen and still at school and had time off from school for the sake of work experience.

When the time came for Alfredo to leave Northampton he went to Cheltenham to be an assistant stage manager there and by that time they were madly in love

There were problems with her family: they wanted their little treasure to be a doctor or lawyer not some one who wiped the arses of actors and who had to work every hour of the day just to make sure some show goes on. But there again her parents didn't know the love and guidance that Alfredo gave her. Didn't know how charming he really could be and, solely according to him, didn't know how good he was in the sack; he winked at me when he told me that bit.

They went to Cheltenham together and he discovered the delights of the locally brewed ales and the lanes and small country roads of Gloucestershire on the back of her motor cycle.

She became so good at her job that she managed to get another job at a theatre in Birmingham. This time she would be the boss and Alfredo went along in his role as her assistant. He didn't have any theatre ambitions just aspirations as a writer. He wanted to learn from the ground up how everything worked but she, even though she was good at her job, was just in love with Alfredo. Hard for me to believe when I saw how he handled women.

It was whilst they were in Birmingham that he lost her.

She was working late at the theatre one night and sent Alfredo home ahead of her. He made his way home by bus to a suburb called Selly Oak and when she started out in the driving rain she was killed in a road that ran through the Queen Elizabeth Hospital. She hit a car head on and even though she was right on the step of the hospital she was dead on arrival.

Alfredo blamed himself for her death. He said he should have waited for her.

She loved the gypsy music of Canada and taught Alfredo many songs. When she died he went to live in Canada for a while and re-discovered the music. Every time he heard that music it made him cry: I rather liked it but I was never sure of his story. He had a penchant for story telling, he loved people to sit around and listen to him but this was something I guess he might have told me about earlier. Maybe it was the reason he had a 'fuck 'em and leave 'em' attitude to the women he met via the newspapers although I didn't see any evidence of that with Leah.

40

When a show moved in to the Henry Fonda Theatre on Hollywood Boulevard two of the cast members came to the house to meet Betty. I was at work when this happened so our opinion – Alfredo's and mine – was not needed this time.

The show at the Henry Fonda Theatre, opposite Pep Boys, was a gay show and involved the whole cast stripping off naked. One of the boys would sleep in Patrick's old room and the other in Betty's. Betty told me this when I came in from work. The first time I saw them was at breakfast the next morning. One of them had bought some lemons and left them on the butcher's block and they were eating bagels and cream cheese when I came into the kitchen.

I introduced myself: one of them was called Gene and the other was Stacey. Stacey was from New Jersey and Gene was from Chicago. They seemed to be nice people and they were as gay as the characters they portrayed in their play.

I could still smell human shit and I mentioned it to them.

"I thought I could smell something when we came to look at the place but I thought somebody had just used the bathroom."

Alfredo came in to the kitchen. All he said was "Who bought these lemons?"

The two boys looked at each other in apprehension.
Gene said "Me."

"Why? There's a garden full of god damn lemon trees out there."

It never occurred to me that there was a lemon tree in the garden but there again I wasn't even sure if they were in season.

I would have introduced Alfredo to the boys but he walked back out. The two boys looked scared.

"When does your play open?" I asked, more to break the ice and ease the tension than anything else.

"Oh.. er next Monday." said Stacey.

Then he rose out of his chair and put his dishes into the sink.

With that Alfredo came back out; he bent down to the pan cupboard and started rummaging about; his arse was facing us, and then he deliberately made a big fuss of turning his arse the other way, in case the boys were getting some kind of treat; why he did this, when he had the most unattractive big fat arse, was beyond me.

The boys could not walk passed him, as he hadn't left much room between the butcher's block and the stove, so they had to wait, tentatively, for him to spend more time than usual looking for the saucepan he found quickly every other day.

They both sat very slowly back at the table where I was sitting.

"You'll have to come and see our show." said Stacey.

"Yes." I said.

When he heard that Alfredo stopped rummaging, stood up and looked at me; then he bent back down and started again.

I didn't talk much to the boys as Alfredo was making so much noise juggling the pots and pans that we couldn't hear each other.

When he found what he was looking for he went to the sink and put the saucepan on the draining board next to it. The two boys got up to go and as they got near Alfredo he turned his arse away from them, facing them as they passed.

They both smiled at him. He gave a forced close mouthed smile back. I ignored his behaviour.

"Can you smell the shit?" I asked.

41

When I came back that evening from work I went around the outside of the house. I wanted to see if I could smell the same shit from there and to see if Betty was still in the guest house. As I got closer I could hear Alfredo's distinctive Dublin voice coming from the kitchen. He was sitting on the butcher's block talking to Stacey and Gene who had brought a friend home. I couldn't quite see the friend but could see Alfredo quite clearly. He couldn't see me so I settled down to listen to him checking that Betty was in the guest house as I did.

Alfredo was like a different man; he was in full voice and was telling the boys a story; as he did so he was gesturing with his hands.

I knew what he was talking about straight away: his trip to Tunisia. He might have told them already about the young man with the shiny boots who followed him but now he was into another episode; he was saying

"They couldn't tell the difference between an Irish and an English accent; they thought I was English. 'Do you like Saddam Hussein?' he said, 'Do you like John Major? Saddam Hussein no attack anybody till

> they attack his country.' Then one of the men said 'fuck.' I said 'that's a bad word to use in front of females' - there were a few women in the shop – I gestured with my hand for them to keep it out."

As he was talking he was using a cod Arab accent and the boys seemed to be loving it; he went on:

> "The penny didn't drop with them that I was Jewish; we had a whole conversation about Israel; they wanted to know what I thought about the Palestinians being banished from Palestine. I said I didn't know anything about it."

Then Alfredo got down from the butcher's block:

> "If I meet John Major I will fuck him,' said the fella 'I will fuck him. John Major does not like Muslims.' As he said this he gestured with his fist like this."

Alfredo made a fist with his right hand and was moving it backwards and forwards like a performing penis.

> "I will fuck him" Alfredo said again.

And he pushed his fist violently backwards and forwards again.

He was laughing and so were the boys.

He went on

> "If he is too much for me to fuck I will use my fist and then my boot."

With this Alfredo lifted his knee up and down to replace his fist.

> "Can you imagine poor old John Major getting fucked by the big Arabs?" he said; then he went to the fridge and took out a big carton of ice-cream.

I looked towards the guesthouse and Betty had just put her light out. When I walked into the kitchen Alfredo had just left the room and I could hear him still laughing as he went to his room. There was still a smell of shit.

42

Next morning I went into the kitchen and a very pretty frail looking boy was sitting at the breakfast table eating bagels and cream cheese.

"Morning!" I said.

A very tiny and squeaky 'good morning' came back.

The boy didn't say anything else; he just sat there. I heard the front door open and Stacey came into the kitchen looking as if he had been to the gym.

"No work today?" I said.

"No! We have a late call. We'd better go."

With that the boy got up from the seat at the table and followed Stacey out and up to his room. As I turned around I saw his plate, with crumbs, and glass on the table. Untidy bastard I thought as I put his crockery into the sink.

When I went into my room Alfredo came in. "I have some rent for Betty" he said "will you give it to her."

"I will not" I said "lost the use of your legs?"

"Ah! She has her shite;" he said "she's fucking anal."

He gave me the cheque.

"I'm not giving it to her" I said "in any case you've put the wrong year on it."

I gave him the cheque back and he left the room. Then he opened the door again.

"Ah go on" he said "I can't stand the old cow; do it for your dad."

He looked at me very sheepishly thinking he was seducing me with his look.

"You're not turning me on." I said "You might if you had a shave once in a while."

"You haven't taught me to shave yet."

"Yet? You keep putting extra words in: we! Yet! Go and correct the cheque," I said "and go out and pay her."

He went. I could see Betty in the garden. She was weeding and had the telephone with her. I called her number "Alfredo is coming out with the rent." I said when she picked up.

"What?"

"It's your lucky day. He's got a cheque for you."

"I gotta go."

She hung up. Then I saw her walk towards the garage and she used the electronic control to zap the garage door open. As it opened she ducked underneath and went into the garage. It was a two door garage; one large one where two cars could park and a single which was the one that Betty had disappeared under; as she did this Alfredo arrived at it and stood there looking for Betty. He looked towards me and shrugged.

"In the garage!" I shouted.

He went to her car, grabbed the zapper and opened the door. As it started to open he ducked underneath it as Betty appeared from underneath the larger garage door as that began to open. So there was Betty standing outside as Alfredo was inside.

It was pathetic.

"He's inside." I shouted.

"I can't help that" she said "I'm very busy. I've got an audition."

With that she went up the steps to the guest house. Then Alfredo came out of the large side of the garage. He looked towards me and shrugged. I had stepped back so I could see him through the lace curtains without him seeing me; he looked up and shrugged but I wasn't there to respond. He climbed the steps to her guest house and very lightly tap tapped on her door.

I couldn't hear anything as a police helicopter came over and drowned out anything he might have been saying. He stood there like Stan Laurel passing the cheque from one hand to the other.

To put him out of his misery I went into the garden, took the cheque from him, went up the guest house steps and stuffed it under her door.

43

I walked around the side of the house again after work to see if I could smell where the shit smell was coming from. Near the front of the house there was a stink of rotting meat and when I got to the kitchen door the smell of shit hit me.

Alfredo was in the story telling mode again. This time he was standing up with the three boys sitting around the tiny kitchen table. Alfredo's hair was wild and tasselled making him look like the wild man from Borneo with his manic dark eyes, dancing around as he spoke and his very black eye brows which he lifted and dropped as he told his story.

The smell of shit was there and he was talking about shit. He was talking about John Major's arse the night before and now he would reach the subject of shit again. It reminded me of the time he had to mention menstrual periods in his screenplay – a need to shock in his story telling. He went on:

"I sat in that disco looking at the ceiling wondering where on earth I was.

I was on the edge of the Sahara Desert with no money in my pockets and with a load of strangers. My mother had just died and I was starting to feel sorry for myself. 'This is how I end up' I thought. Then one of the Scottish sisters came up to me and asked if I wanted to dance which cheered me up. Made me feel attractive again, you know: wanted.

Before we knew it everybody wanted to go. I went into the jax but it was busy and when I came out they had all gone. I dashed out into the car park and there they were getting into a taxi. I opened the back door and dived across the back seat. Everyone laughed! The driver didn't seem to mind and we took off. Archie was in the front with the driver when one of the Arabs shouts something and we stop at this kind of café in the middle of nowhere. I thought they were closed but the Arabs knocked the door. About two minutes later the door was answered and we were all in there and they were putting the chips on for us – you know the fries.

I still needed to go to the loo and I asked them where it was – well to cut a long story short I got into the loo and it was as if somebody's arse had exploded; shit all over the place – devastation. Shit up the walls - all over the broken loo. So I left it and went for a walk up the road a piece to go in the bushes. I walked about fifty yards away and whilst I was up there three motor scooters arrived. Three of the local jet set and one of them was the fella in the flashy boots that had followed me; the fella with the Gucci watch."

So he had told them about being adored once. I couldn't wait any longer outside so went in. Alfredo stopped talking when I came in but I just waved and went to the bathroom. I thought I would leave Alfredo with his audience and called my mother in Dublin; she didn't mind me calling her early. She didn't seem to be making sense when I had spoken to her earlier so I wanted to make sure she was all right; she was as clear as a bell and we had a long talk about old times and NYPD Blue.

When I got back into the kitchen Alfredo was sitting by himself; his audience had gone to bed.

"Did you get dinner?"

"I went to the pizza factory." I said.

"You need to get some vegetables down you," he said "vegetables and fresh fruit."

44

The message from Betty the next morning surprised me; she mentioned that the rent had been paid and said she knew that something was probably coming to her as she had seen a letter arrive from Alfredo's father after hearing him on the phone asking his father to send money, but she went on to say that Alfredo had been frightening the boys with his story telling and would I tell him to stop. Frightening the boys? I was quite impressed with the performances. It brought him to life and all thoughts of his depression and wanting to commit suicide at Stinson Beach seemed a million miles away but he would already know this news as he would be sitting on the can in the bathroom listening to Betty leaving me the message. They both probably knew that they didn't have to tell me anything, nor did I have to pass any message on, as they were eavesdropping on one another: he knew she listened to him on the phone to his family, or whoever, and she would make her telephone call to me each morning she was home within earshot of the bathroom where Alfredo had settled himself on the throne after being disturbed from his nightmarish slumber by Betty's daily call from the living room to her congressman; so I didn't say anything as I knew he got the message. I didn't like it though as I didn't think he was doing any harm. When I came in from work that evening there was no Alfredo telling stories and no boys there to listen. They were doing the gay play at the Henry Fonda Theatre but the house still smelled of shit.

The smell of shit was all over the house. You could smell it in the kitchen, the bathroom, the back garden – everywhere. And nobody mentioned it;

maybe it was just me; maybe it was the devil as I'd heard that's how he smelled.

The next morning I went into the bathroom and the smell was as bad as ever. After I had a pee I flushed the loo and there was a kind of bubbling. It seemed to be flushing but not flushing properly and the water, instead of emptying the pan filled it. So I re-flushed and pieces of faeces came up. It wasn't mine - it wasn't labelled but I knew it wasn't mine. So I filled a jug of hot water and flushed it down the loo. That only added to the water; the shit stayed where it was: floating on top. I knew that there was a plunger in the cantina and as I stepped out of the bathroom to fetch it Alfredo came out of his room:

"You can't go in there just yet." I said.

"Why not?"

"There's a blockage."

He tried to push passed me.

"You can't go in" I said "there's a blockage."

"But I need to go."

"You can't go. Stand here and stop anybody going in."

That seemed to do the trick. I had given him a job and he felt needed.

I used the plunger in the lavatory but it was useless; no water went down.

"I need to go" said Alfredo "I need to go somewhere."

"A big job or a little one?"

"A little one now. But I'll need to go later."

"Go upstairs."

He screwed his face up.

"Go upstairs" I said "they won't bite you."

He started up the stairs and stopped half way.

"You never know" he said.

"Go on!" I said and he carried on.

When I went back into our bathroom it seemed that the water had gone down very slightly so I got into the shower hoping it would have taken care of itself by the time I finished. After my shower the water had gone down only another one eighth of an inch. I thought that if I flushed again the plug may open and let the water out or it may overflow. Neither thing happened. When I flushed the lavatory the water level rose to within an inch of the top.

I tried the plunger again – no good.

So I went outside and got the high pressure hose pipe. Then I went into the bathroom and opened the window so I could feed the hose through. When I walked back around to feed the pipe through the window, Alfredo opened the bathroom door and put the fan in there to stop the smell spreading throughout the house. This caused the bathroom window to slam shut.

So I had to go back outside and push the pipe through the window again.

I took Alfredo to the tap in the garden so he could turn the water on when I wanted.

I shouted "Are you ready?"

"What?" He said

"Get ready to turn the tap on."

"The what?" he said "The tape?"

Ever loving lovable and helpless Alfredo was beginning to get on my nerves. So I shouted "The tap! Why would I call it a tape? Whatever you want to call it! The fucking faucet whatever the fuck you call it. We're supposed to be running water through the hose."

When I looked out of the bathroom window he was nowhere near the tap. I went out and stood him by the tap and told him to wait there until I said 'Go.'

I put the hose down the lavatory and shouted through the bathroom window for him to put the water on.

Nothing!

I stared at the top of the lavatory pan with the water one inch from the top. Nothing happened.

No noise.

So I went to the window.

"Go Alfredo for fuck sake."

The water started.

Nothing happened apart from the water getting higher.

As it got close to the top I shouted stop.

It didn't stop.

I shouted again "Stop! Stop! Stop!"

The water overflowed onto the floor taking a good measure of shit with it.

Then I ran out and into the garden.

"Off, off off!" I shouted.

"Oh!" he said and turned it off.

"Fuck it, shit for brains."

When I said that he wandered off:

"I've got more than shit for brains."

"Whatever you have for brains don't go into the bathroom."

He stopped walking and turned to face me.

"Can you get the mop and bucket?" I said to him.

He stood there like a spoiled child.

"Can you get the mop and bucket?"

"Please." he said.

"Please. Now fuck off and get it."

I was fond of Alfredo, but he was reacting like a cat or dog that didn't know what was going on and who wanted its belly rubbed. He had no sense of urgency whatsoever and the only thing on his mind or his only target was that he wanted his shit in the place he normally did it and he didn't want to be delayed.

When he was looking for the mop and bucket one of the boys came out of the kitchen door; it wasn't Stacey or Gene but a friend of theirs. At first I thought he had come out to help – maybe there was plumbing in his family, who knows?

Wrong!

He passed by me as if I didn't exist, went straight to the garden swing and lay there in the sun, exposing his shaved, but very white body, to the ultra violet rays as if he hadn't a care in the world; which he hadn't; he didn't give a fuck about the little crisis we were having and as I looked at him I thought maybe I should go to the movies and leave them to it; 'Casino' was playing and I wanted to see it.

Alfredo brought the mop and bucket to me but it was full of tea leaves as Betty had been saving them for the garden. She said they were good for her roses and that's where I threw them; onto the roses. He stood there as if waiting for my next order: "Thanks very much" I said, "I appreciate it. Sorry I shouted at you."

We were living in the house so in a kind of a way it was our business but if we were in an apartment block we would have simply called the manager who would have seen to what needed doing. We could have joined our friend in the sun or gone to see 'Casino' but then the shit would have been piling as high as the house.

I mopped everything in the bathroom as best as I could; the water had subsided but the smell of shit was dreadful; I went to work.

The next day Gene came down the stairs and said:

"My toilet is blocked."

I couldn't believe that we were having such a big shit crisis and it had been going on for days. Gene asked me where Betty was and I told him to try the guest house which he did. When he came back I asked him what she had said:

"Nothing really."

Nothing really! What was that supposed to mean?

I looked into our bathroom and the bath tub had excrement in. That was beyond a joke and I wasn't going to stand any more of it, but when I got to the guest house Betty wasn't there. She had gone out with Harold. I hadn't heard his car but she had gone and left us to it knowing that we were bound to sort it out.

I got the high pressure hose again and put it into the bath tub but it didn't do any good; it only added to the problem leaving a load of brown water in there.

Then Gene came into the bathroom and said Betty had been on the phone to say that she had been in touch with a plumbing company that would come and use a rod to clear whatever obstruction was there. She said she had left the number by her phone. So I called the company and they did indeed remember Betty's telephone call but said they wouldn't come out to the house unless we paid up front. So I asked Alfredo if he had any money and he told me he hadn't. I told him I wasn't going to pay – I don't think I would have got it back from Betty – and told him that I would take a crap at the local coffee shop every day and shave at the office before I paid anything out.

Gene came to the rescue and said he would pay the one hundred and seventy nine dollars to the man when he came out. So I called the company and put an 'Out of Order' notice on the bathroom door. When Alfredo saw the notice he said "What happens if I have to defecate?"

****

45

"Is there a bathroom in the Guest House?" said the man from Dyno-Rod.

"Yes." I said.

"Can you flush it real quick?"

This, he said, would give him a clue as to where the problem lay. He had taken the top off a large cover in the garden and was inside it and when I returned he asked me to go to the bathroom in the house and try that one.

I went in there and Alfredo had taken a shit. A lot of the water level in the lavatory had gone down but there was his shit; he had left it there like a cuckoo laying an egg in a strange nest.

I flushed it and was very lucky that the water stopped just short of overflowing.

"That's better," said the man from Dyno-Rod, "I think it has something to do with the new bathroom in the Guest House."

Alfredo came into the garden "Is it okay if I do my laundry" he said.

"Don't be silly." I said.

"I have to do my laundry."

"But you only did it last week."

"I have some more."

"Let's get the thing fixed first," I said "Be realistic."

"Somebody's been using kitchen roll." said the man.

I looked at Alfredo and he shrugged.

"Can you flush the one in the house again?"

"I'll take care of that." said Alfredo.

As soon as he said it I knew it was a mistake. Stacey came out of the kitchen door, whilst I waited for Alfredo to return, carrying a bottle of sun tan lotion. He smiled at me as he went passed to join his friend on the garden swing.

'We have a major disaster." Alfredo called from the kitchen door.

This didn't surprise me one little bit. I had a feeling when he said he would take care of that that that would not be taken care of and that that would be something else to worry about.

I went into the bathroom: the loo had been full of his shit and he had flushed the loo and the shit had risen over the top and was all over the stone bathroom floor and on the carpet in the hall.

"What shall we do?" he said.

"There you go with the 'we' again.

I left him to it and closed the door.

"Betty left you with the responsibility," he shouted "and I should sue."

I went back to him in the bathroom.

"Sue? Who are you going to sue? Out of order means out of fucking order; nothing more and nothing less. Now it's your shit so clean it up."

As I walked away he called me back: "I'll need a dust pan and brush."

"What for?"

"To shovel the faeces."

"Shovel it into the loo. It'll be fixed soon."

"I'll shovel it into the bath."

"Listen," I said, "this fucking muesli, garlic, basil, oregano and oatmeal flavoured shit is all yours and it's all over the place and the whole fucking house smells like shit so clean it up."

I didn't mean to let him have it so violently verbal but I did and his face just squirmed.

"Okay," he said very meekly.

The man from Dyno-Rod was watching Stacey rubbing sun tan lotion onto his friends back as he lay in the sun; his friend had shoved his shorts right

The man from Dinorod was watching Stacey rubbing sun tan lotion onto his friends back as he lay in the sun; his friend had shoved his shorts right up his arse so as to expose himself to the sun.

"All fixed" said the man, making no mention of what he'd been looking at "All fixed and all guaranteed as long as nobody uses kitchen roll."

"We need to get a water pump" said Alfredo when I got back inside.

"We don't need a water pump," I said "and I'm sorry I shouted at you."

"Okay." he said and went back into the bathroom.

I sat in my room and called my mother in Dublin but the smell was so bad that I took my phone into the garden and smoked a cigarette as I spoke to her.

Stacey was getting sun tan lotion rubbed into his back as I spoke to my mother and the thought did cross my mind as to what she would think if she knew what I was looking at. She was up late in Dublin watching the TV and she sounded very sleepy; maybe I'd woken her up. When I came back in I heard Alfredo struggling to get out of the bathroom.

"What's the matter?"

"I'm locked in."

He had found a key on the window sill and used it. It was an unwritten rule in the house that we didn't lock bathroom doors and this was probably the reason why. The key was so old and the lock so old that they were not expected to work. I went around to the side of the house and as the bathroom window was some way from ground level I got the steps from the cantina and climbed up to Alfredo who opened it. The window was too small for either of us to get through, especially Alfredo, but I could see quite clearly as he tried to turn the key in the lock.

"It's not your day is it?" I said.

He looked at me shamefacedly.

"Mind you don't break the key in the lock."

"That's what I'm frightened of doing." he said.

I asked him to pass the key to me as it would probably work if I tried from the outside. Failing that he would have to stay in there or knock down the door. Fortunately it worked from the outside and when it was done I put the key down a drain in the street in front of the house.

Stacey was still getting massaged with lotion by his friend as I returned from the street: "What's happening?" he said.

'Nothing." I said as I took a last drag of my fag before going back to my room.

The next morning Alfredo had disappeared.

46

I knew he had disappeared mysteriously because he had left his computer, his 'complete works floppy disc' as he called it, and I could see that his bed had probably not been slept in. He was in the habit of making the bed as soon as he got out of it and throughout the day he would climb up and sit on top of it leaving various marks on his duvet; the marks on the duvet were still there from the day before.

I had gone into his room to apologize for losing my temper and when I realized he was missing I felt guilty. I could still hear the constant ticking of something that sounded like a clock and I could see his things spread about: his collection of pens, hardly any of them in working order; his walkman, a thesaurus and dictionary, a book of Shakespearean sonnets and an old birthday card. They had a kind of pathetic look to them as they lay there waiting for their master's return.

I wasn't sure what to do about his computer, as he was still in the habit of carrying it around with him, but I knew he had paid some, if not all, of his rent to Betty so maybe I needn't have worried.

His car wasn't in the street so maybe he had taken the long drive to Stinson Beach to end things. I somehow doubted it; I was sure that if he ever did

commit suicide that it wouldn't be on the spur of the moment; it would be carefully planned and carried out with the utmost of planning. But I couldn't figure out why he had defecated at that precise time: when there was a stranger working on the plumbing, the other lads in the house and he was bound to know that it would overflow and if not seen by everybody then certainly smelled by all and sundry.

Maybe he needed to do it for some reason. He was always talking about reaching rock bottom so he could start again. He wanted to be broke so he could go onto the streets and beg but he didn't have the nerve when he tried it out the night I first met him. Maybe he felt something similar about his shit? Maybe he wanted to get down to basics again and let everybody see it like it was when he was a baby? Who knows?

Betty was away with Harold and there was no one else in the house so there was no one to tell. I went into the garden for a smoke and to think things over. The dog next door looked at me as I sat there with a 'take me for a walk look in his eyes.'

Alfredo was the only person who ever took the dog for a walk. Its owners took him to the grassy knoll at the top of the street but that was about it. Alfredo would take him to dog shit canyon . . . Dog Shit Canyon? Maybe that's where he was?

It was quite easy for me to get there and it was a pleasant Sunday afternoon when I started out. All I had to do was to get the bus from the bottom of the street and get off a few stops further from Highland Avenue and go up Vista Street.

The corner of Highland and Hollywood was usually very busy with traffic and people walking about; mostly tourists. They had plenty to choose from with the 'Chinese Theatre,' 'The Hollywood Wax Museum,' 'Ripley's Believe it or Not Museum' and a host of street entertainers usually dressed to look like old movie stars. One thing that amused me was the fella that was supposed to be Charlie Chaplin was taller than I was; in fact he was taller than most people.

Two stops after the urban Hollywood and Highland junction I got off the bus at Vista Street to a different world. There were plenty of posh houses and, even though it was winter, there was still the hazy summer feeling of Hollywood. Something about the Spanish type of buildings reminded me of old Hollywood with William Holden face down in a swimming pool – now where was that? Miles from where I was. The part of Sunset Boulevard where that film was set was some way into Beverly Hills and instead of movie stars living there then the place was inhabited by Attorneys, lawyers and the like; oh Jayne Mansfield's big pink house was still there on Sunset Boulevard and it was owned by Engelbert Humperdinck.

By the time I reached the top of Vista I was fighting for breath; I couldn't believe that Alfredo climbed the hill every day – or every day he came with the dog – but then I realised that he would drive up to the gates of the canyon.

There seemed to be a choice of which way to go when I got inside the gate. People either walked to the right or to the left. I decided to go to the right along a narrow pathway with a kind of meadow to my right and some trees to my left. People were walking along wearing head phones listening to music which struck me as odd; they had obviously come to the canyon to experience nature and they blocked out its sounds. I heard 'knock knock knock' – sounded like a woodpecker. So I looked up to see if I could see anything. The sun streamed through the trees and didn't blind me too much when I saw it; a little bird banging its beak on the tree. People walked passed me in their baseball caps, some swinging their arms to add to their exercise and one or two running but no one took any notice of the woodpecker. I don't suppose a country boy would have taken much notice but it was the first time I had seen one with the naked eye.

When I got to the bottom of the little pathway I could see that there was another gate to my right. People were walking in from that gate and going passed me or to my left which, presumably, was to the top. I looked up – it was. I could see and smell why Alfredo called it Dog Shit Canyon.

I turned to the right and went to the other gate and could see Fuller Avenue outside.

Turning back in I saw a sign warning me about *Rattle Snakes* but nobody else seemed too concerned as they walked their dogs so I didn't get worried. The only snake I had seen since arriving in Los Angeles was the one underneath Christine's car.

Just inside the gate to the right, just after the Rattle Snake sign, was an old man with a few things spread out that he was selling: cigarette papers, little pieces of *Indian Jewellery*, Mexican bracelets and other trinkets. I described Alfredo to him as best I could but he didn't seem to know. The man seemed to be in another world, maybe the nineteen sixties, and had a glazed look in his eyes.

There was nothing else I could do apart from walk over the canyon and see if I could spot Alfredo.

There was a winding road which was overlooked by trees. I had visions of them shooting westerns up there in the old days. I could see where Hopalong Cassidy might have caught up with the bad guys and where the Indians might hide behind the rocks; Indians who were probably white men dressed up but that was old Hollywood.

After about ten minutes I reached a plateau and stood with a group of people looking out over Hollywood.

"What's with the tennis court back there? I asked.

I had passed an old dilapidated tennis court with sunken nets, broken fences and grass growing through the cracks.

'Errol Flynn used to play there' said a young girl hardly old enough to have even heard of him.

'Oh' I said.

"Yes he used to live there in the old house."

There were some steps just inside the gate near to where I had pondered a left or right turn and that, apparently, was the remains of an old house.

But the girl was wrong; Errol Flynn only came to stay and play tennis. Sir John McCormack, the Irish tenor, bought the house originally.

The next bit was very steep in fact it was a real climb. I almost had to touch the ground with my hands to get up. When the really steep bit stopped and it kind of levelled out a bit I could see where I was heading: a very long steady climb up to a bench at the top.

To my left, as I climbed up, was a drop into the canyon and it was quite possible that Alfredo has fallen or jumped down there. But there were too many about for him to do this and I had spotted that the place closed at sundown. Then it was left to the coyotes and rattles snakes. The coyotes would cry en masse whenever they heard the siren of a police car or emergency vehicle and being Hollywood that was not a rare thing.

On the way out I checked in the vicinity of Fuller Avenue for Alfredo's car as I had checked Vista on the way up but it wasn't to be found.

47

I didn't plan to tell Betty about Alfredo's disappearance so when I got back to the house I went into his room and put the little light on next to his bed so that she would think he was in when she got back from her weekend with Harold.

Gene was in the kitchen and I asked him for a lift up to Griffith Park; that was the only other place I could think of to look for Alfredo. I don't even know what I was expecting to find and just felt a bit guilty, I suppose.

He had a convertible and we drove with the top down to Griffith Park which wasn't very far. The car had been left to him by a friend who had died of AIDS. I didn't pursue the subject; I figured if he wanted to talk about it he wouldn't need my prompting.

"What happened to Alfredo" he said.

I didn't know if he was referring to him being missing so I just said "In what way?"

"He started to tell us stories in the kitchen in the evenings and then one night he just stopped. When we saw him again he wouldn't even say hello."

"Didn't one of you complain?"

"Complain?"

"Yes" I said "Betty said he was frightening you."

He laughed at this.

"Frighten us? We were enjoying his stories. He's quite a story teller - why would she say a thing like that?" he said.

"Beats me."

And it did beat me.

The car park at Griffith Park was full. Gene looked around for a place to park.

"You don't need to hang around" I said.

"It's okay, man" he said "this place looks cool. Hey! Look at James Dean. He was bi-sexual too."

"Are you bi-sexual?"

"No" he said "I'm full blown gay – I was referring to Alfredo."

"Wow! You think so?"

"Yes. We got the impression he was. He mentioned a rich Arab that pursued him in Tunisia."

"The guy with the metal toe caps?"

"Yes" he said "it was the way he described him. A nice little ass, is how he put it."

"He didn't describe him like that to me." I laughed.

"Well he wouldn't to you, would he, you're too straight!"

Round by the main observatory building we could see the sculpture of James Dean.

"Over there, man, look!"

He pointed to the wall by the observatory steps and it was where they had filmed the knife fight scene for the movie 'Rebel without a Cause.'

A family car pulled out from a line of cars and Gene made for the space.

Most of the people there were Latinos; they were making their way back to their cars after family picnics carrying ice boxes and portable furniture; some of the smaller children were being carried by their daddies with their mothers following behind pushing push chairs full of picnic and barbeque equipment.

"Maybe you see bi-sexuality where I don't?"

"Maybe' he said "– takes one to know one you mean?"

"No" I said "Alfredo's a writer. He assumes certain opinions and attitudes to see what the other fella thinks."

"He spent the night with the rich Arab."

"He what?"

"He spent the night with him."

"Did he tell you that?"

"Yes. He didn't say they slept together - Let's go and look at James Dean."

"You go" I said "I have something to do."

I walked to the cars and he followed.

"What are you looking for?"

I told him about Alfredo.

"That's okay" he said "I'll help you. But let's look at James Dean first."

We looked. It was useless. Alfredo's car was nowhere to be found and the park itself was many many acres and far too many acres for us to cover in a month let alone a Sunday evening; it was beginning to get dark and it would be Alfredo's second night out and missing.

Gene knew he was missing and I did and no one else on earth either knew or cared. Just as I had suspected earlier: any of us could go missing and not be missed.

We drove back to the house and he told me more about Alfredo's Tunisian adventures.

"I heard him telling you about the motor scooters showing up at the chip shop."

"That's it" he said "that was the night."

He was alone in Tunisia and got involved with a Scotsman called Archie. This was a big Glaswegian boy in his thirties. He wasn't a skin head he was more thinning on top, which was how he put it.

Archie was on the run. He had been arrested for drunken driving in Glasgow and on the day before his court case he took a flight to Tunisia on a package trip - you know for the one price you get your hotel and fare in one for a fixed time."

"I'm familiar with that." I said.

"Archie's time had run out in his hotel so he was looking for somewhere to sleep and as Alfredo had two spare beds in his room he let Archie have one for a couple of nights. He said he didn't get a wink of sleep as Archie snored the night through.

On the night of the motor scooters coming to the coffee shop he had gone up the road a piece because the bathroom was out of order; when he got back Archie was standing outside saying he'd got no money and didn't want to get involved in buying food and said he wanted to go back to the hotel. Alfredo was after an adventure and gave Archie the key to the room. He said it wasn't far to the hotel and knew the way back so Alfredo let him go and joined the younger crowd in the coffee shop.

There he met the guy with the Gucci watch; he spoke English having been to school in England and Alfredo found him charming.

They were all Muslims so there was no chance of a drink and that was the real reason Archie had gone back to the hotel as he had left a bottle of whiskey in Alfredo's room. In fact he had a few bottles in there as he sold them for forty pounds each the following day as whiskey was hard to get.

So they all had a good time and at the end of the evening – which in fact was early morning - Alfredo ended up on the pillion of Mister Gucci's Vespa.

He took him back to a very large house a few miles away which was

Gucci's parents' house and he was very well looked after; they ended up having breakfast together in Hammamett.

He didn't say he had slept with him – on the other hand he didn't say he hadn't."

Alfredo hadn't told me about that bit – he told me about admiring the Arab horsemen on the beach and the Gucci guy following him around Hammamet but he told me he knew where his sexual preferences were when the pen swapper's sister had cornered him in the shop.

It was none of my business – I had taken on the responsibility of looking for Alfredo as I thought he was in trouble but I couldn't help thinking of one thing he had said to me: 'it would have been ironic if I was gay and let an Arab arse bandit fuck me.'

48

It was quite dark by the time I got back to the house. Betty was in the guest house and I had a look in Alfredo's room just in case he had returned. As before: the silence of the room apart from the ticking of the clock; the squeaky floorboard and the emptiness and abandonment; his things lying about the room; the banjo I had played, the guitar neither of us had; his computer sitting on the desk waiting for a click on the keyboard to bring the monitor to life; that's what gave me hope: the fact that he had left things expecting to come back to them.

Something was making a noise near the monitor; I know now that it was on standby but then I thought it was on and ready to start any minute. I half considered trying to turn it off but changed my mind. I put the bedside light out and turned his television on. Then I put another light on. There was a British programme on KCET which is the local Public Broadcasting Station and so I decided to watch. I sat down in Alfredo's favourite chair and sat on some papers. They were under the cushion and I fished them out. There were two sheets of foolscap paper and I read the typed script:

> 'I am a writer; I have written a lot; I write every day of my life: I get out of bed in the morning and crash into my keyboard and start to write; I write anything; when people look at me this is what people see.
>
> I am scared and lost – I need help….please.
>
> Sometimes I find it hard to write – like now – I am finding it hard because my thoughts are going round and round; I spent half an hour trying to decide whether to write around and around but I settled for round and round as we can see; because my thoughts are going round and round I can't communicate them to anybody. It was always easy to communicate but now it's hard; I mean what thought do I communicate to my mate?
>
> This is what people see.
>
> I am a writer and I am good. I see things in English literature that no one else understands or even begins to comprehend; I see the shit, the stomach, the colours the music and I saw them before someone else pointed them out to me in Ulysses; my purpose in life is to pass this on and since I discovered my purpose in life I feel like I am in another world. People don't always understand me and what I am doing, so it is easy for me to be by myself then I can get work done.
>
> I work hard because I have so much to do but it affects my sleep as I find it hard to shut my mind down; it goes on and on and spins round and round and stops me sleeping. It used to be that I would go to sleep

as soon as my head touched the pillow but not now.

I always thought that the others saw the things in literature that I see but when I pointed little things out to them they looked at me as if I was mad – so now I keep things like that to myself. I talk to people less. I don't want them to think I am dangerous or should be locked up so I talk to people less.

But that's okay by me!!!

I started hearing what I thought were voices about a month ago but now I am starting to realise that I have always heard voices. – I just thought that other people were hearing them too.

So that proves to me that I am different and that I have to work very hard to appear normal but I am not sure how long I can keep it up – I think I need help.'

All of that was in one sheet of paper. I put that underneath the other sheet and started to read that:

'Now the countdown begins – it begins for me and me getting help!!!!! This time in two weeks time – three hundred and thirty hours and fifteen minutes from now I will be sitting in the doctor's office.

I mean it will happen SLOWLY – day by day, minute by minute and not forgetting the hour by hour as the hours are as important as the minute minutes – but it will COME!!

The point is I have survived so far and I will survive henceforth and now I feel a bit of motivation – NOT TO QUIT FIGHTING these voices that tell me to DO IT DO IT yes!'

Poor Alfredo . . . ..

49

There were two new messages on my voice mail service when I woke. I had hoped one of them might have been from Alfredo but they were both from Betty. I had forgotten to listen to the one on Sunday morning so I listened to the two of them together. She blamed Alfredo for hiring the most expensive Rooter Company, as she called them, and she said that he hired them on purpose as they were the most expensive. She also told me that he had fallen behind in his rent again and wanted me to have a word with him.

I ignored both messages, went to the garden for a cigarette then took a shower and left for work. It was earlier than usual but I figured I could look for his car from the bus on the way in.

The search for him now took on a new meaning; I wasn't qualified in any kind of mental illnesses but the words on the paper frightened me. Hearing voices was schizophrenia and schizophrenia started in young men which meant Alfredo had been suffering from it for over forty years or so. If he had been suffering from it all that time he had kept it from me possibly through drugs. I knew he was paranoiac and suffered from depression but if he was off the pills for schizophrenia he could be dangerous and I didn't know what to do.

Alfredo had spent two nights out; it wasn't exactly the North Pole, and people living in cold countries would laugh at anyone complaining about being cold in Southern California, but the temperature was around forty-eight degrees Fahrenheit and unless he was in his car he would be exposed to a certain amount of discomfort. I could see the in the distance the bus coming but I decided to let it go and head back to the house to see if his pills were in the usual place.

On the way back up Maltman I passed Betty coming the other way carrying her broom; ready to sweep the twenty yards or so of Sunset Boulevard she devotedly did every Monday morning.

50

When I got back I found his medicine in the usual place. I don't know what the pills were for – they *could* have been for schizophrenia I didn't know; all I knew is that he hadn't taken them with him so unless he had a spare set he would be in the same state as he had been the time he had tried to come off them before; he would have the shits, pins and needles and whatever it was that ailed him.

I put his light on to keep up the pretence. I didn't want Betty to find out he had gone as I think she might have hired somebody to dispose of his belongings and maybe try to rent the room to someone else. Who could blame her? I didn't want her to see the papers I had read so I hid them under the duvet; I did not want her to find them and get them analysed and find she had rented her room to a psychotic.

I got off the bus earlier than my usual stop and went to see the Schlepper in his office on Hollywood Boulevard. It was the usual seedy and dark walk up although I could have taken the lift. But what was the point for one floor?

As I approached the door of his office I would smell his cigar. The same cigar, no doubt, that had permeated the house the day Patrick burned Alfredo's papers in a pathetic show of stupidity.

"Come in!"

The same untidy office with papers all over the place and piles of actors' head shots on the chairs greeted me as I entered. He seemed pleased to see me and offered me a seat after clearing a chair of the head shots and putting them into the waste paper basket.

"Don't worry about the poor actors" he said "I'll take them back out of the trash when the seat becomes vacant." He shrugged "Then I'll look at them and put them back into the trash – oye why do I bother?"

I sat down; "Have you seen Alfredo?"

"What's up?"

I told him; I didn't say anything about the papers I'd found.

"What makes you think I know something?" he said.

"You're the only person I know that knows him" I said "I have heard of someone called Morton but that's about it."

"Morton! I heard of Morton but I ain't never seen him. Do you know anybody that's seen him?"

"No" I said.

"Fucking right! He don't exist – or maybe in the imagination of Alfredo – as you call him."

"What do you call him?"

"Me?" he said "I call him a jerk. He can't make up his fucking mind whether he's a Jew or a Mick. I know what I am – I'm a Jew and you're a fucking Mick."

"Thank you" I said.

"You're welcome. He's probably lost in a shit pile of ice cream somewhere. How the fuck he got to write that play – part of a play – about James Joyce is beyond me – what there is of it. If he ever finishes the fucking thing – and I think it's a big fucking 'if' – maybe he's gone off to write it somewhere?"

I left the Schlepper to his life and went to work hoping that there would be a message for me at the office from Alfredo.

51

Of course there were no messages from Alfredo. I tried to settle down and work but I couldn't get him off my mind. I still felt guilty and decided to take the rest of the day off.

As I was walking passed the first place I ever bumped into Alfredo I thought of Leah; maybe he had gone to see her and asked her to put him up. He had said he was going to help her the next time she went to the Pasadena Rose Bowl flea market. And who was this person – Milton or Morton or whatever his name was? Alfredo mentioned him nearly every day in conversation; sometimes he would say Milton and other days Morton; maybe this was his imaginary friend?

Back at the house I looked through the papers on Alfredo's desk and couldn't find any address book or evidence of Leah's telephone number or address: there were various notes, small dramatic scenes, experimental dialogue, some notes about Indians, notes on Irish Jews and some newspaper clippings about the slain Prime Minister of Israel Yitzhak Rabin; but nothing about Leah.

Then a thought crossed my mind. His telephone with the big dial buttons was there so I picked it up and pressed the button for last number dialled.

After a few rings a voice answered; a very familiar voice: "Hello" she said.

"Hello Betty" I said – I had to think quickly "Could you go into my room and see if I've left my cheque book on the desk – I think I might have lost it."

"Hold the line" she said and I could hear her walking from the living room to my room, opening the door and going in. After a few seconds, which seemed like many minutes, she went back to the phone.

"Yes it's here": she said. "Are you at work?"

What could I say? "Yes."

"You're speaking very quietly."

'Yes" I said "We're not supposed to make personal calls."

With that I hung up.

She put the phone down and walked to the front door passing within a few inches from where I was standing.

What was Alfredo calling Betty for – maybe he had left a message?

Betty walked to the mail box and as she got there I went out of Alfredo's back door and towards my room. She had left the door to my room open so I couldn't stay in there. I went around to the living room and noticed that Betty had closed the front door behind her so I ran towards it and saw her going down the side of the house and as she disappeared behind the building I opened the front door and went out and walked down Maltman towards Sunset. I passed the gap between our house and the one next door and saw her walking towards the guest house at the back carrying the mail.

Maltman descends towards Sunset and then ascends again on the other side leaving Sunset Boulevard in the dip. As I walked down the hill I was sure I could see Alfredo's car parked facing up the hill on the other side of Sunset;

I walked towards it and the closer I got to it the clearer it became that it was, indeed, Alfredo's car.

He was lying across the back seat; I tried all the doors but they were locked. The keys were in the ignition so I banged the windows to try and wake him up; there was no response. Was he dead? Was he in a coma?

I should have smashed the windows straight away but something told me that he hadn't finally killed himself. I banged all the windows, doors and roof to try to wake him but he didn't stir. I shook the car violently and it was moving him about in the back seat. He wasn't waking up so I picked up a brick and smashed it through the front passenger window. The glass shattered over the front seat.

"Alfredo! Come on wake up!"

There was a terrible smell of piss and Alfredo had snots and saliva around his mouth and nose but, at least, he was alive.

He started to stir and I shook him again.

He mumbled something.

I sat him up slightly and put my hands under his arm pits and struggled to sit him up.

"Come on – come on" I shouted at him and I managed to get his head and torso out of the car door.

Then I pulled him again and his legs dropped to the kerb like a dead man his feet underneath him. I pushed his feet away from him with my foot then I dragged him on to the pavement.

A Mexican girl of around twenty five came out of one of the houses and came to us. Alfredo was not awake and his head started to sink onto his chest.

"I'll get water" the girl said and went back into the house.

I slapped Alfredo's face gently a few times but he hardly responded.

His trousers were wet with piss and his white hair was wet and flat on one side of his head and sticking up on the other. He was a very sorry sight and I wondered what I was going to do with him.

The girl came out again with a basin of water and a glass. Together we sat him against the car and I held his face up as I slapped the water over it. The girl put some water on to a cloth and wiped the snot and saliva from his mouth.

"Come on, Alfredo" I said "I'll have to take you to hospital. . ."

The girl put the glass to his lips; he sipped.

"Not too much" she said.

When he heard her voice he opened his eyes and stared at her without saying a word.

"Come on, drink" she said.

He did what she asked him and sipped at the water.

"I feel terrible" he mumbled.

"Let's get you into the car and I'll take you home" I said.

"Do you have far to go?" said the girl.

"The other side of Sunset" I said, "I'll have to do a 'U' turn."

"I will come with you."

She couldn't sit in the front passenger seat because of the glass so she got into the back. Alfredo would like that even though he smelled like a public lavatory. As I drove I could see him quite clearly in the rear view mirror and he looked almost drugged. It was only a very short drive and when we were walking him up the path at home Betty came from the side of the house.

I held him upright and told the girl to go and open the never locked front door.

"I'll take you to the bath room" I said.

"No! Take me to my room."

"You're going to the bathroom' I repeated and we, more or less, frog marched him there up the pathway.

As we walked Betty stood watching us. The house still smelled of shit but the Mexican girl wouldn't notice as Alfredo stunk worse.

I sat him on the lavatory seat. "Let me go to my room." He said.

"Everything in your room is fine" I said "I've been making sure it was ok."

"Can I get anything for you?" said the girl.

"No thanks" I said "You get back to your house – and thanks very much."

"Okay" she said "I'll call in tomorrow to see how he is."

She went out. Alfredo was displaying the withdrawal symptoms from his medication as he had before. He was cold and shivering.

"I'm sorry" he said.

His eyes were closing and opening and he had a problem focusing.

"I'm going to put you into the shower" I said "I won't take your clothes off – I'll just sit you in the bath and turn the shower on."

"No" he said "leave me for a while. I'll be okay."

"What got into you?"

"I needed to get away" he said "Nothing was going right. I made a fool of myself, I can't pay my way, I might as well not exist."

"I went up dog shit canyon to look for you."

"Dog Shit Canyon?" he mumbled. "I used to go up there and forgive everybody for being nasty. I would forgive Patrick his stupidity, meanness and vanity. I would forgive his cruelty."

"His cruelty?"

"To his wife – he abandoned her. Walked out on her and then sued her. I used to forgive Betty every time I went up there. She woke me up every morning with her loud phone calls – and I think she did it on purpose and then she would call you and say nasty things about me. I would go up the canyon and forgive her. I forgave you your stupidness for not wanting to play James Joyce for me."

I smiled to myself. I hadn't closed the bathroom door and when I turned to do so Betty was standing in the doorway.

"Oh?" I said.

"Do you need any help?"

"I'm going to run some water onto him," I said "But thanks."

"I'll be in the living room if you want me. I thought you said you were at work!"

She went and closed the door behind her.

I managed to take Alfredo's jacket off fairly easily but I needed help to remove his boots; he had them tied in complicated girly knots:

"I'm going to have to cut these off." I said.

"No" he said "They're only tied."

I tried to untie them but they were too complicated for me.

"I'm going to get a blade," I said and went to my room.

As I walked away I could hear him say 'oh no.'

There was a fairly sharp razor blade on my desk so I took that back to the bathroom together with some of my towels. He had fallen forward by the time I got back. He was still seated on the lavatory seat so I straightened him up.

"Come on now," I said.

I cut the laces from his boots and pulled them off. His feet stunk to high heaven and I pulled his socks off too.

"Come on now" I said "up you get" and I gently eased him into a standing position.

"Now you are going to fall if you don't snap out of it' I said.

"I'm not getting in there," he said.

"Yes you are," I said.

I lifted one of his legs up and put it into the bath.

"No!" he shouted and pulled it back out.

"Do you want me to get Betty?"

"No. And I'm not getting in there. I don't like showers."

"I'll get Betty," I said.

As soon as I said that he lifted his leg into the bath again, then the other one.

"Ok, sit down." I said.

He put an arm on either side of the bath and very tremblingly eased himself into a sitting position. I turned the shower on and aimed the water jet from the shower at his face.

"Oh no" he said.

Soon the water started to soothe him; he closed his eyes and let it hit him on his head flattening the white hair which was still fairly matted. His khaki shorts were stained with urine and the water from his head trickled onto his shorts getting rid of some of the stain and sending a brownish stream down to the bottom of the bath and down the plug hole.

I opened the bathroom window, lit a cigarette and blew the smoke out as he lay there. I wasn't going to strip him, I figured I would leave him for a few minutes and let the water clean him up as much as it could with his clothes on.

After one last deep drag into my lungs I dowsed the cigarette in his shower before putting it into the waste basket.

He was gently sleeping as he sat in a tiny reservoir which was slowly getting deeper.

"Time to wake up, Alfredo." I said

No response.

"Alfredo?"

Still no response as I turned most of the hot water off.

"Hey!" He screamed as the cold water hit him "Hey! Turn it off."

"In a minute" I said as I turned the rest of the hot off and let the cold water hit him. He was trying to catch his breath.

"Okay okay" he said "Okay I'll get up."

The cold water was almost like a switch which brought him back to life. I turned the water off and he started to shiver.

"Come on" I said and I gathered the towels together putting a smaller one over his head.

He started to dry his hair which stopped him shivering. I could see that I might get some sense out of him so I asked him if he wanted me to take his wet clothes off "No! No!"

"Okay" I said "I'll be back in five minutes" and I left him to it.

I went onto the front porch and sat on the swing for a few minutes and smoked another cigarette; it felt good although it really was time for me to quit. When I got back to Alfredo he was sitting on the lavatory seat wearing my towel robe. He looked a lot better already and there was a flush in his cheeks which, with the few days beard growth, made him look like a tramp. I picked up his pile of clothes.

"Leave them" he said "I'll see to them later."

"I'll see to them now" I said and I picked them up and took them out to the washing machine.

"I am two people" he said when I got back "the person awake and the person asleep. The person awake can be very rational when he is left alone by the person asleep. The person asleep has fantasies, bad dreams and nightmares and he influences the person awake so that the person awake doesn't always know if he is the person asleep or not.

I dreamt I had a huge penis: a huge huge penis - maybe eighteen inches long. It wasn't hard or anything and I wasn't sure what I was going to do with it but then the person awake took over and woke me up. I needed a piss. So the person awake was telling the person asleep to wake up and piss.

The person awake was off duty yesterday or he had gone from me and didn't wake me up so maybe I wasn't the person asleep either. If you had left me there maybe I would have died and if that is what death is like I don't mind. It might improve me as a writer to be able to write about death and it may be the answer to my play.

You see I can't write it till I know the truth. That's what I am waiting for.

I used to go to Bewley's coffee shop in Dublin and just hang around the writers and actors in the hope . . . . . "

He just trailed off and sat there looking at the floor.

"In the hope of what?" I said.

"Nothing," he said "Nothing! Thank you for your help."   With that he got up and walked to his room.

"You can wash the towels when you feel better" I called after him.

"Okay" he said as he went into his room.

I followed him in: "What about your medication?"

"What about it?"

"Are you going to take it?"

"No" he said as he turned his computer on.

52

The next day, before I went to work Leticia knocked the door. Leticia? She was the Mexican girl who had helped me with Alfredo.

"How is he?"

"He's coming along." I said.

Alfredo had taken the dog for a walk whilst I was in bed then he had gone through his usual routine and was working at his computer.

"Would you like to see him?" I said and I called in through his door:

"Someone to see you, Alfredo."

"Who is it?" he called.

"Come and look."

This brought him to the door. Leticia's eyes lit up when she could see he was okay. He was clean shaven and his white hair glinted in the sun as he bent forward to shake her hand.

"Thank you for your help." He said.

"You're welcome." She said.

There was a slight silence.

"Good to see you looking so well."

Then there was an awkward little moment for Alfredo as he didn't know what to do or say.

"I need to finish my .. er.. I have to something to finish." He said.

"That's okay. I'm glad to see you are okay."

He went in after a few more groans. I looked at her – she was fairly attractive..

"Sit down." I said.

I pointed to the swing and she sat on it.

"I have won two tickets from the radio to a show at the 'Whisky-a-go-go."

"You won two tickets; that's great" I said "What did you have to do?"

"It's not a competition – I'm a member and I called in for the two tickets. Would you like to come?"

I thought for a moment; why not?

"When is it for?"

"Friday; we're seeing the Super Chunks."

53

I half expected Alfredo to be in a subdued mood but when I went in to his room he seemed quite chirpy.

"Taking the little Mexicano girl out are we?" he said.

"She's taking me out." I said "How are you feeling?"

"I'm okay. It was . . . I don't know; something I needed . . I got into the car and drove up to the other side of Maltman. Then when I got to the top of the hill I turned around and I was going to drive straight across Sunset without taking any notice of the traffic lights; I figured if I could survive that, with the odds totally against me, I was meant to live."

"What happened?"

"I chickened out. When I commit suicide it will be on Stinson Beach or somewhere else as tranquil."

"Were you feeling ashamed?"

"Every animal likes the smell of shit and we're no exception. We don't go around smelling each other's arses but we like the smell of our own farts. We eat the insides of fowl with *foie gras*, which nearly tastes like shit; we eat Stilton cheese, which smells of arseholes – we love our dirty insides. These fellas are eating each other's shite."

He was referring to Gene and Stacey.

"That's not fair." I said.

"Ah I'm only joking. I nearly went through with it though: I called Betty and asked if she would take me on as a manager for this building. I would be able to collect the rents, do some handy work and be generally in charge of the running of the house. But then I remembered how you looked at me when I suggested it to you."

"What did she say?"

"It was the answer phone. I was going to come down that hill flat out and if it wasn't for the Joyce play I think I might have gone through with it."

"How are you getting on with it?"

"I'll start next week. I have a little job to do for the Schlepper first."

****

54

So he was back on form again. The ritual started the next morning with him almost falling out of bed and landing in front of his computer screen. The fact that he was back into the old routine meant that everything else fitted neatly into place: Betty called the Congressman and would wake up Alfredo in the process; then she would go into the garden and call me from outside the bathroom where Alfredo would be listening to her phone call. She never mentioned the incident of Alfredo going missing and that she had heard Alfredo mention that he heard her complaining to me. She just got straight on with the rent payment she wanted from him.

The dog from next door was happy again; Alfredo took it out for walks up to Griffith Park or Dog Shit Canyon and I was starting to cough a lot because of my smoking, I suppose. I promised my mother that I would give them up but it was easier said than done.

By the time Friday came around when I was due to go out on my date I was feeling rough. If I was in Ireland I would have walked down to the doctor but America isn't like that. If you have no insurance you wind up paying around one hundred dollars just for the consultation. I got off the bus one stop before the Whisky-a-go-go and lit the inevitable fag. It stopped me coughing as I was coughing up quite a bit of phlegm. I could see her waiting for me outside Duke's coffee shop which is next door to the Whisky. I wasn't sure if it was a thing of kindness she was doing for me or whether we were going out on an official date. Maybe it would have been a good idea to see her on a regular basis so I could learn Spanish from her. She looked quite tasty waiting for me and as soon as she saw me her face lit up with a big smile.

"I have the tickets." She said.

I flicked my cigarette into the gutter and we went in.

55

I never quite figured out the reason Alfredo took a crap on top of the very high water in the lavatory that day. He must have known what was going to happen when the thing was flushed. Maybe it was like some kind of cuckoo dropping an egg into the nest of another bird except that instead of a bullying chick we got a bullying stink. It was in our nostrils from the time we woke to the time we slept; even when I was at work I still imagined I could smell shit. It might have been some sort of experience thing when he wanted to do something to see how other people reacted so he could put it into his play. I'm not sure how that would fit into his play about James Joyce? In the four days since he had come back he got back into his routine of writing. As soon as he opened his eyes he would climb out of bed, put the computer on and go and listen to Betty bad mouth him over the phone to me; then he would get on with his work. Maybe his work involved some woman bad mouthing somebody and he would use what Betty had said in her daily tirade? I didn't mention the papers I'd found. I was waiting for the right time.

The Whisky-a go-go was packed as the band playing was very popular. The Super Chunks - and my joke about them having pineapple testicles didn't go down well with Leticia. But we had a good time. It gave me an excuse to dance and by the time I finished dancing my shirt was stuck to me as I was sweating so much. She was a good dancer and I just kind of moved around with her and tried not to make too much of a fool of myself. But it was hot and getting hotter. There seemed to be a swirl of smoke and a powerful pong of the mix of a thousand and one bottles of cologne, scent and after shave lotion. I was expecting Alfredo to be ill after his experience in the wilderness but he was never better. His eyes looked clear, he shaved every day and even his hair, though it was still wild, looked good; the sun seemed to shine off it which gave him an inner life.

When we came out of the Whisky I felt terrible. It was very late and I didn't fancy getting a bus. I shouldn't have done it but I lit up a cigarette. The smoke went straight down and made me cough. That was unusual as it usually cleared a hole for me to breathe through.

"You shouldn't be smoking if it makes you cough" she said.

"Yes I know"

I flicked the fag into the gutter. God I felt awful. We crossed the street to get the bus and it must have been our lucky day; Gene was driving east on Sunset and that's what we wanted. He pulled up at the lights and called to me.

"Do you want a lift?"

We did and we got in. Leticia got into the front and I sat in the back.

It was my first experience of cruising along Sunset Boulevard on a Friday night. It was like a scene from the movie American Graffiti. Los Angeles' rich parents had let out their young and let them use their very expensive cars and limos and they had gathered that night to block and delay my way home.

I tried to sleep as Gene drove us through the mayhem but the fact that we were in a convertible meant that every one could see me and every one thought that I was drunk. There were so many comments about me that I didn't bother to open my eyes after a time but I could hear girls giving their cell phone numbers to guys in cars going in the opposite direction. Girls were sitting on the top of their hired limos – sitting on the roof with their legs trailing down through the sunshine roof. Inside the limos they appeared to be having parties and the girls on the roof would change places with their companions now and again and go back inside the vehicle to party.

I was quite envious of it. Envious of their age, as I thought I was too old for it, and envious for the fact that it was just beyond me.

It took about an hour to get through the two hundred yards or so of Sunset Boulevard but after half an hour I dozed off. When I woke up Leticia was gone and Gene was helping me into the house.

56

I didn't need any help getting to sleep that night. The next morning Alfredo woke me up. On a small saucer he had about four or five pills and a glass of water.

"Drink this"

I did and went back to sleep.

This happened lots of times and I got out of bed once in a while for a pee which came out almost gold as it was so yellow. Alfredo said it was the pills he gave me which was causing the colouration of my pee and after a few days of tender loving care I wanted to get out of bed which I did and went straight to the kitchen. I didn't bother with my towel robe; Betty would be out, so I went to the kitchen as I was.

Alfredo was mixing his usual concoction for breakfast.

"Ah ha – Lazarus awakes" he said.

I sat down at the table.

There was something strange about Alfredo. He was putting loads of herbs into the oatmeal he had cooking on the stove. Then he put loads of sugar; that was something I hadn't seen him take before. He had his back to me and that was when I discovered that he did voices on the radio. I had always wondered what the guy who read the advertisements on NPR looked like and it turned out to be Alfredo. Whenever I tried to start a conversation he would put his hand up to stop me talking and say in a high pitched voice: "w.w.w. dot Schwab dot com" then carry on talking about something else. He could do loads of voices and demonstrated them for me. I was going to ask him if he could get a job for me doing voices on the radio but he just started talking in another voice. Once or twice he sounded a bit like Donald Sutherland.

Later on that day he said he was going out drinking and I just sat in the kitchen and waited for it to get dark. I didn't want to move as I didn't want the excuse to smoke. I knew I had some cigarettes in my jacket pocket but I didn't want to be tempted so I sat in the kitchen. Pretty soon I could hear Alfredo walking very slowly around the side of the house. Then I heard a laugh – a female laugh. I looked through the window and I could see he was very unsteady on his feet and he was being held up by Betty who looked just as drunk. She was laughing at him every time he tried to say something. He had his arm around her and they were holding each other up. This was new to me. Maybe they'd been doing this behind my back all the time? Maybe that was why he called her just before he went missing?

I went to the back door and peered around the wall. I didn't want Betty to see that I wasn't dressed.

"Oh my God" he said when he saw me "Hang on! Hang on! I'll be all right in a minute. Jasus what's that?"

He was trying to step over an imaginary lump in the path; I stood there looking at him as he talked.

"Oh! Aright. Yes aright. Wha? Yes. Alright, yes that's it, alright. All-all right. Yes. Now where the fuck . . .where the fuckarewe? Wha? Handymountstand? Hough? Wha? Oh. Sandymount Strand."

He sat down next to the big bin. Betty tried to sit on his lap. I didn't move. It was fun to watch them like this.

"And wherethefuckis tha . . Wha?.. wherewhat?.....Bloom had a wank – is it whank with an aitch or wank without one? Now, hold on. Who had a – I think I must be sober . . so I must be sober to think so I am asking who . . . who is Bloom? I need the room I'll rent it to Bloom. Okay: here we go. Let us have a . . . who were those people and where am I . . I am in Sandymount cove . . is that right? I am somebody and I am having a whank. If you're in Dublin you will speak with a double U aitch sound: a wa huh!

They say in Inverness and Dublin the English 'she is spoken best.' Lie back."

He lay back on the front lawn. Betty lay next to him.

"Sandymount Cove! I remember the Middle Arch on the north side. Now that was over the road from where Don Cass lived and Mrs Curtis who was his aunt – I remember the middle arch. We used to swim at the middle arch. We used to go there with our nicks and get in."

What was he doing on my side of Dublin? I knew Don Cass and Mrs Curtis too.

"I remember one day we went for a swim. I went for a swim with my pals and we got stripped down to our nicks – that wasn't at the middle arch that was at Dollymount. They had these big lumps of concrete called changing rooms which is where we had to get changed and when I got to the bench some fella had left his clothes on one of the benches and his underpants were full of shite."

That happened to me. But I couldn't remember telling Alfredo.

"Full of shite they were. Hang on there's something coming. . . a cab . .a taxi.. fuck Bloom and his whank and your man with the shite in his . . bloomers . . bloomers? Is that what they were?"

Then he started to shout very loudly:

"I need to go to Ballybough . . yes Bally . .no hang on Fairv. . . no. . . Donneycarney."

The louder he shouted the louder she laughed and the louder she laughed the higher her skirt would ride up exposing her underwear. Pretty soon you could see her waist at the top of her drawers as she lay there giggling like a school girl.

I went up to him to try and stop him shouting. I held his shoulder and he looked at me and started to do one of his voices: "This is Bob Edwards" he said "and you're listening to *Morning Edition*."

I laughed then I opened my eyes and looked at the ceiling. I didn't know how many days I had been asleep but the radio was playing just as it had been when I went out with Leticia on Friday evening.

I got out of bed and put on my towel robe. I hadn't smoked for the time I was in bed and I didn't crave for one either. When I reached the kitchen Alfredo was mixing his usual concoction for breakfast. It was just after eight-o-clock; very early for Alfredo. He looked at me with shock as I walked in. I must have looked a sight with a few days growth of beard: "What day is it?"

"Tuesday" he said "You've been asleep since Friday night."

I had woken up quite a few times during that time. I was wide awake once in the dark but eventually went back to sleep.

I sat down at the table.

"Thanks for looking after me" I said.

I felt confused.

"I called the office for you – told them you were sick."

'Thanks!" I said.

"I spoke to the schwartzer."

I looked at him quickly. He was winding me up.

"I told Christine." He said.

I smiled.

He started to get some herbs and cinnamon together for his porridge but then changed his mind. He took the oatmeal and put it onto a plate and gave it to me.

"Here" he said.

Then he put a jar of honey and a banana next to the bowl.

"Eat this. It'll do you good; *Earl Grey* tea?"

Then he put the herbs and cinnamon into the remainder of the cooking porridge for himself.

57

I got to like the mixture of porridge with banana, raisins and honey washed down with a cup of *Earl Grey* tea. When I had finished breakfast Alfredo went out for a walk with the dog and he returned at midday.

Then it was time for him to prepare lunch for me. He seemed a different person when he had some one to look after and he gave me breakfast, lunch and dinner for the next couple of days.

He told me that Leticia had been to see me a couple of times but I didn't remember anything:

"She helped me give you a bed bath" he said.

"Fuck off" I said.

On Friday I felt a lot better and went to work; I had to as I didn't get paid for time off.

Alfredo almost gave me the third degree before I went out of the door making sure I was up to it "are you sure you don't want me to take you to work?" he said. He was like a mother hen but I was fine and got on with my day.

When I got home that evening Alfredo was gone; as soon as I walked through the front door it was quite obvious: his door was wide open and everything he owned had been taken from the room.

I walked in and there was no sound of the ticking clock, no lap top computer, no telephone, with its giant buttons, no nothing and no Alfredo.

Harold was busy putting Betty's goodies into the large fridge when I got to the kitchen. He had to move out of the way when Betty came in from the back garden with a pile of bed sheets.

"Excuse me, Harold" she said "can't you see I'm trying to get passed?"

He stepped back and let her by without saying a word and carried on with loading her fridge. She would probably find more goodies in there in future as Alfredo would not be around to take a chocolate bar when he fancied.

Betty nodded to me as she passed.

"What about your buddy?" said Harold.

"What about him?" I said as I sat down. I felt like going in to the back yard for a cigarette but suppressed the urge.

"Taking off like that." He said.

"First I knew about it." I said.

Betty came back into the kitchen and when Harold saw her coming he stepped back to let her proceed to the guest house.

"Paid his rent in full and vanished." said Harold.

Betty mumbled something as she went passed.

"Is some one else moving in?" I asked.

"Not yet" he said "Betty is moving in to his room for the moment."

Oh dear; I knew that Alfredo had been a pain in the arse with his occupancy of the bathroom but Betty was an equal pain with her cold water conservation: leaving dishes under taps to catch the drips.

There was a coffee shop around the corner. I decided to go there for dinner.

When I got back to the house they had gone off for their weekend so I wouldn't have to share the bathroom and the ground floor with her for a couple of nights. The boys were off gallivanting somewhere after their show so I had the house to myself for most of the time. They would come in way after I had gone to bed and stay in bed for most of the day.

The next day I walked down to see Leticia to thank her for coming to see me. We went out to Griffith Park and wandered around with many other

Latinos. I had another look at *The James Dean Sculpture*.

Over the next few weeks it wasn't much fun knowing that Betty was in the next room. I felt obliged to keep my radio down. The fact that Alfredo had left didn't stop the morning phone messages. She went from moaning about Alfredo not paying his rent to moaning about the fact that he didn't give her enough notice she felt she was entitled to a further month's rent.

This happened every day for the next couple of months. Christmas came and went. My mother was disappointed that I didn't go home for Christmas. I spent it with Leticia. Her family was in Mexico so we went to the Laugh Factory for the free meal. It was a very nice gesture by the owner and was aimed at actors but anybody showed up with a lot of down and outs with comedians trying their shtick.

We went out a lot of times together; lots of movies and once or twice to a few Hollywood bars. Neither of us had a car so we had to take a bus at all times of the day and night.

One night after a late night at The Room, a bar in Cahuenga, we caught a bus along Hollywood Boulevard: the usual motley crowd of passengers. We managed to find a seat together behind a woman of about sixty five, wearing a pair of Levi jeans with a skirt over the top. She had very short bleached hair, a very very Southern accent and she was carrying a bundle of plastic shopping bags.

She turned around and looked at me. Then she looked at Leticia. It was not a look of approval. I was expecting some kind of racial slur but she said:

"What time is it suh"?

"Twelve-o-clock."

"Twelve? .. My!"

A small time went by and I asked myself what I was doing riding on a bus in Hollywood at midnight. It was a fairly dangerous place to be at any time of the day but Leticia didn't seem worried. Twelve-o-clock in Hollywood is eight in the morning in Dublin and Dublin would still be going on the same as any other day. There was a fella called Pickard who used to go into the country where people said he used to fuck sheep; he would bang my door every morning at eight. My mother would shout that I was in bed and I wondered at that moment if he was still banging the door or even fucking sheep.

A black man at the back of the bus wanted to get off so he pulled the bell and started to walk towards the front. As he got near us the woman stood up and nearly touched him as he went passed.

"Don't you touch me you big black motherfucker nigger yuh." She shouted.

"I didn't." he said.

"Get the fuck out of my face 'fore I get my pistol out at yuh."

The man didn't know what to do. He looked at her and started backing towards the front of the bus; fright in his eyes.

The woman was struggling with her bags trying to unzip the zips.

"You motherfucker nigger! I have mah pistol here an you gonna git it now."

I thought of poor Pickard with the sheep with his bang bang bang on the door at eight each morning and there I was on a bus in Hollywood with some other nutter. At least Pickard was harmless.

"I'll kill you yuh motherfucker!" she shouted again.

I thought if Pickard was still knocking my door my mother would be telling him that I don't live there any more and that I was in Hollywood on a bus listening to some poor demented woman who was bound to have a silver looking pistol in one of her bags but when I looked around the bus nobody seemed to be trembling in their boots and those asleep stayed asleep.

The black man got off the bus but this didn't quieten down the ballet dancer in the aisle who's shit and belongings were scattered all over the place: bits of cigarette packs, bits of paper, bits of matches, receipts from every shop she'd ever been in, as she was shouting to the man through the window:

"Motherfucking nigger: I'll get that motherfucker. You think I'm crazy 'cos you know he's gone?"

I didn't know who this was addressed to as I wasn't looking at her.

On the bus came another black man. He was a little confused. The nut case looked at him. The man went towards the back of the bus and shouted to the driver to stop that he needs to go the other way. He went towards the driver and as he moved so did the Madwoman of Chaillot who almost brushed passed him and almost touched him.

As the man talked to the driver she shouted at him:

"You motherfucker nigger think you can touch me?"

This man was able for her. He stopped talking to the driver and gave the woman a hard stare. She stopped any noise and sat in her seat. He got off the bus. She looked at him as he walked along the street.

Before the bus started up the driver spoke into the loud speaker "Lady! Will you clear up that mess?"

The woman didn't move.

"Lady!"

The woman started to clear up the mess.

I looked again at Leticia and she didn't seem too bothered; nevertheless I started to think about buying a car; I also thought of Pickard in Dublin fucking the sheep and I wondered if he ever wore a condom.

****

58

Half way through January my phone rang at work and it was Alfredo. I knew he would call eventually. He was on the phone to me for almost half an hour. He didn't tell me where he was and he wouldn't give me a number. He said he would let me know that all in good time. He wanted to talk about his suicide. I said I nearly felt like committing suicide when I found out I'd been abandoned. He liked the joke and I told him if he wanted to commit suicide that he must find a way to enjoy it.

"You're always saying that" he said.

"I mean it. Don't kill anybody else doing it but if you really want to do it jump off a big building and enjoy the fall - or drive a fast car over a cliff – enjoy the fall."

"I saw somebody throw himself off the bridge in San Francisco" he said.

"Did you?"

"Yeh; I was up there contemplating it; just looking out looking at the water; in my own misery my own mind; and next to me was another fella and he was looking – he was looking too. I was aware of him because I thought he was watching me; making sure that I didn't jump. We were there for about - I don't know - maybe half an hour, forty five minutes, something like that – next thing you know, up he gets and over he goes almost as quick as that; and down he floated; and that's what he did he floated. He seemed to go down very slow and when he was half way down he seemed to turn, he turned and floated down on his back; and then he hit the water. It must have taken. . . it must have taken about five - five or six seconds – maybe even ten seconds I don't know – it took all that time for him to fall. And that's when I changed my mind; I wanted something instant."

He went on to say that he didn't care about enjoying anything any more and that he wanted the pain to end then he hung up. There was no automatic star sixty nine at the office so it was a waste of time trying to call him back.

Maybe two weeks later I got another call from him. By this time I had bought a car. I bought Leah's Chevy Nova. She called me about Alfredo and after we talked for a while I found out she wanted to sell her car. It cost me five hundred dollars which I thought was a good deal then I had to go to the Department of Motor Vehicles and pay them a percentage of what I had paid for it even though it was a private sale.

Alfredo was just around the corner from where I lived. I got the address from him and drove around there. He made me promise not to tell Betty. When I got there I met the wild man from Borneo. He hadn't shaved since he had left Betty's house. He had put on quite a few pounds too and was sitting on a futon looking like a beached whale. He had finished the script and wanted me to read it.

"I'll take it home with me' I said.

"No" he said "I want you to read it here – out loud to me. I need to hear it. I need to hear it in your voice."

"I'm not playing it" I said.

"No I've given up on you – they're going to get somebody that was in the Love Boat."

"The Love Boat?"

"It was a TV show here."

"What's his name?"

"I've forgotten, but it'll come to me on the night, I'm sure. You may be able to do me a favour."

"I'll read it but I'm not playing it on the night."

"Why not?"

"I have never worked in front of an audience."

"Okay" he said 'Okay. Do you want a cup of *Earl Grey*?"

"Yes please."

"If you go into the kitchen it's all there for you."

"Cheeky buggar – what kind of a host are you?"

"Go and fill the water from the flask out there. I have this."

He had a quarter pound tub of Haagen-Dazs ice cream in front of him.

"This'll do me," he said.

I went into the kitchen. There was a thermos flask of hot water, some *Earl Grey* tea bags and a mug for me to use. I made a cup of tea and I went back into him.

"Why have you let yourself go?"

"I needed to work" he said.

"You need to lose some weight and - shave."

"I haven't been out since I came here. There's a guy here who does my shopping; the laundry is just over the street. I'll be alright for the show; it's next week."

"Have you been on to them?"

"Yes" he said "It's all under control."

His script wasn't clipped together so as I read it I put the page I had finished on to the futon next to me. We were on either ends of it as there were no chairs in the room. On the front page it said The Man with the Pen, by Alfredo Hunter . . .

"Zurich: the evening of January 12th - 13th 1941.

Music: the haunting theme 'Love's Old Sweet Song' on CD.

As the music continues the house lights begin to dim and when they are dark the music fades slightly as a voice fades in:

VOICE OVER

Once upon a time, and a long time ago it was, in the city of Dublin, in the land of Ireland, there was a man with a pen."

He interrupted me there: "That's the bit I want you to do."

"What?"

"That line there: Once upon a time, and a long time ago – et cetera."

"That wasn't in before when I read it."

"There's a lot in there that you won't recognise – but I want your voice reading that first line."

"I can't do that . . ."

"You can;" he said "we'll record it. It'll be on a loud speaker."

"Where?"

"I know a studio - the Schlepper fixed it up for me. You'll be okay."

"Okay" I said "do you want me to carry on?"

"Yes please: from the top."

"Music: the haunting theme 'Love's Old . . . "

"No – start with Once upon a time" he said.

"Or once upon a tome" I joked.

"Ha ha very funny" he said "now let's get on."

He didn't say that nastily and I didn't want to upset him so I carried on:

"Once upon a time, and a long time ago it was, in the city of Dublin, in the land of Ireland, there was a man with a pen.

The music continues to play.

A voice mumbling and moaning is heard - almost incomprehensibly.

VOICE

.....I was yours and you were mine and I was fine around that time and I was finding you my time and I was fine and........... "

"What's all that about?" I asked "Is it Finnegans Wake?"

"No and it doesn't sound like it either. Listen: it's the last night of his life; he's delirious – he's asleep . . . . it shouldn't really be clear . . I were yourn and doo were bine er . . .but it would be easier for me – for this exercise if you just read it and didn't ask questions. Will you go again?"

"From the top?"

"From the top. . . . once upon a time, - and try not to read too many of the stage instructions: I know the play; I wrote it."

I laughed.

"Once upon a time, and a long time ago it was, in the city of Dublin, in the land of Ireland, there was a man with a pen.

The music continues to play.

A voice Mumbling and moaning . . . sorry!" I said to Alfredo.

".....I was yours and you were mine and I was fine around that time and I was finding you my time and I was fine and........... "

AND THEN Ogh! Ooooooohghhh! PAIN

THE LIGHTS FADE IN AND A MAN CALLED JAMES JOYCE IS LYING DOWN AND IS IN GREAT PAIN TO THE BELLY. HE TURNS OVER AND SITS UP ON THE SIDE OF THE COT WITH HIS BACK TO THE AUDIENCE.

Ooohhh! Nora – Giorgio - where are you?
HE STANDS UP . . . . "

59

It was beautiful. There is no other word to describe the play.

I read all the parts in the same voice: the person playing Nora would also play Joyce's daughter, Lucia, and various other female walk-on parts; the person playing Joyce would only play the one role but would talk about others and assume their dialogue.

When I finished he said "thank you – I needed to hear it."

I looked at him sitting on the edge of the futon and tried to think how something so beautiful could come out of something so vile; he looked awful with his full beard and long white matted hair.

He knew that I was impressed although he didn't say anything. There was a look of achievement on his face and he sat there in silence. From the moment I read 'curtain' which was the end of the play we didn't speak a word after he said thank you. Not for a full two minutes. Eventually he said:

"Do you want another cup of tea?"

"Yes please' I said and I went to make a move but he said: "Leave it to me I'll get it."

He struggled to get up. This wasn't the Alfredo who took the dog out every day and walked like a prize fighter – this was an old man.

He came back with the tea.

"You're going to have to get some exercise" I said "you can't be this weight."

"Them days is gone, Joxer" he said "maybe forever. My exercise was only for this play. Do you remember the tree in Ogden?"

"Yes" I said "The two esses?"

"The two jays." he said "Well I went there a few times with the dog, when we had been up Dog Shit Canyon; it was a great inspiration to me. I would get the dog to piss up that tree: for luck."

I had to laugh at this.

"It's true," he said "how's the old bag?"

"The dog?"

"No the dog is fine, I know that; the lad that does my shopping had a look in there a few times and told me. How's Betty?"

"She misses you."

"Misses me! Look at this lot."

He picked up some post cards. They were pictures of Betty when she was slightly younger and starring in a soap opera.

"They're all the same!" he said "I get one a week."

I looked at one and there was a message on the back asking Alfredo for one month's rent in lieu of notice plus payment for the plumbing repair.

"She sent them to her own address and they were redirected on to me by the post office. The woman is mad. It wasn't my fault the sewer blocked it was her badly built guest house. It overloaded the system. She needs certifying not me."

I drank my tea and thought maybe he was right. I had heard the same diatribe every morning on my answer phone.

He approached the subject of schizophrenia in the play as James Joyce's daughter, Lucia, suffered from it later in life after a tormented childhood. I wanted to ask him about the papers I had found but decided against it.

60

A few days later Alfredo called and told me where I had to go to record the voice over for his play: it was the Musicians Union Studio on Vine Street. There was a very big room, like a school theatre with a stage, and in the middle of the room there was a box I had to go into; a kind of booth: Alfredo and the engineer became voices in my head. It took about one hour to do. I did it every way possible: more accent, less accent, clearer, bringing up the inflection at the end, dropping the inflection at the end; it didn't mean much to me I just struggled on with it and felt totally incompetent by the time we were finished; eventually it was in the can and they came out and thanked me. They had to knit it together, as the engineer put it, so I left them and went to work.

The night of the show eventually came around and after I paid what seemed to me an absolute fortune to park the car, I got to the front of the theatre. There were quite a few people standing outside and one of the first people I saw there was the Schlepper. The obligatory cigar was in his mouth as he surveyed the scene. When he spotted me he came over and shook my hand.

"How are you?" he said as he took the cigar from his mouth.

"I'm doing very well."

"Alfie was saying you were sick!"

"That was a couple of months ago;" I said "Alfie?"

"That's what I call him. I never figured out whether he was trying to be Spanish or Italian using a name like Alfredo."

"It's a very common name in Dublin." I said.

"Is it?"

I wasn't sure if he believed me or not but I shook his hand and went inside. Alfredo was standing in the foyer. There was a look of excitement in his eyes. They seemed to be dancing and they glistened with the bits of moisture that were gathered in the corners.

"Patrick's here." he said "He's after his money."

I laughed.

"The first thing the gobshite said to me was 'when am I going to get my money?' I said he'd get it after the show."

"Will he?"

"He will in his hole; but it'll keep him here till the end."

"Are you coming in?" I said.

"Not on your life."

He had shaved but his hair was still very long. It was clean but Alfredo looked very old. There was a lot of flesh under his chin as if his face had lost weight and left the skin sagging. It wasn't exactly a dewlap but it was getting that way. The rest of his body was flabby and filled with ice cream and when I saw him walk it was as an old man.

I went inside: the place held about one hundred. I was told afterwards that it was a ninety nine seat theatre. They were called Equity waiver theatres where actors could perform without the union insisting that they get the minimum pay. All other union rules had to apply and actors used them for showcases to try and get Steven Spielberg to watch them perform.

Patrick was sitting at the front. I could see his grey hair straight away although there seemed to be something different about it. He would usually have his hair combed over to the side, as with most Americans of his age, and, as it was getting a little thin on top towards the front, his pink scalp could be seen. I couldn't quite see the front of it but for some reason I thought he was wearing a wig. When I looked closer I was almost sure.

I sat down at the end of one of the rows on the right.

After a few minutes, when every one had taken their seats, the lights went down and a version of 'Love's Old Sweet Song' played in the blackout. Then the lights came up slightly and we could see the silhouette of two people sitting on chairs. The lights stayed in the same place for a few seconds then my voice started with the recording I had done for them.

'Once upon a time . . '

I felt quite vulnerable even though I was sitting in a black out. It seemed to go on forever and when it had finished the lights came up and the two people on the stage read the whole play. They were both American and tried some kind of singy songy Irish accent. I didn't recognize them from the Love Boat, or whatever they had been in, and I missed the first few minutes of the play. I kept thinking about my voice and didn't listen to them reading the lines for quite a few pages. I had never really heard my voice being amplified before and as soon as I heard it I knew why Alfredo asked me to do it.

Eventually the play was over and there was a tremendous round of applause. The two artists on the stage took many bows and then some one from the audience shouted 'author.' Then another voice called 'author' then another and another.

He deserved it and I shouted it too. Of course, Alfredo was nowhere in sight. When the shouting for author had died down the Schlepper dragged a protesting Alfredo through the door.

"Here's the author" he shouted.

The audience burst into applause again and Alfredo reluctantly took a bow but he wouldn't get onto the slight stage.

When I met him in the foyer he was on a wonderful high. He was being worshipped by all and it was almost impossible to get him to listen.

I shook his hand and he threw his arms around me "Thank you" he whispered "thank you. It is all down to you."

"Don't be silly" I said.

When he pulled back there was a tear in his eye.

"This is the director." he said and he introduced me to a tall man.

The director shook my hand and then shook Alfredo's hand. They didn't say anything to each other. A woman came up to the director and two or three people tried to ask Alfredo something. The woman that came to the director said "What war was it set in?"

Stupid question, really, but I wasn't prepared for the answer: "What war is it, Alfredo?" shouted the director.

The noise level was very high with all the talk and Alfredo couldn't hear him.

"I thought you directed it?" I said to the director.

"What?" he shouted.

"The second world war!" I shouted back.

He turned to the woman and told her.

I could see that Alfredo wasn't enjoying it any more. He was surrounded by people and then I saw Patrick approach. He was, in fact, wearing a wig and he came by me.

I clapped him on the shoulder.

"How are you doing?" I said.

"Didn't understand a fucking word!"

"What – the play?"

"Yes the fucking asshole – he can't write about the Irish."

"It's brilliant," I said – he really annoyed me with his comments.

I tapped the director on the shoulder. He turned around.

"You should meet Patrick Conroy - he's an actor."

I could see he really didn't want to meet another actor but he said "Of course."

"This is the fella who directed tonight's show."

Patrick's eyes lit up and they shook hands.

In the background I could see the two stars of the show and they were giving autographs.

I pushed passed them and grabbed Alfredo and pulled him gently outside.

"Thanks for that" he said as we reached the street.

The Schlepper was standing there smoking a cigar.

"Good job." He said.

"You weren't in there." said Alfredo.

"I know but I read it a few times."

"You didn't read the latest draft."

"I know but I trust you."

He shook Alfredo's hand warmly "I got to go." said Alfredo.

"Okay:" said the Schlepper "We'll talk."

Alfredo turned and shook my hand then he turned it into a big hug. He didn't say anything he just walked off.

As he walked along the street the Schlepper said "Off to a mountain of ice cream."

He looked like a very old man as he made his way to the end of the street and his car.

We could hear his car coming out of the car park and as he appeared in the street mountains of exhaust fumes filled the air. He drove passed us and waved. As he did so Patrick came out of the theatre and said "Where's Alfredo?"

"There he is." I said and we watched him get to Hollywood Boulevard and turn right.

Patrick watched him go.

"You should meet Alfredo's friend. The Schle. . . I'm sorry I've forgotten your name."

"Milton."

Milton?

He looked at me and winked. Was he the infamous Milton or was he giving Patrick a false trail to stop him bothering him in the future?

"Milton: meet Patrick. Patrick's an actor" I said to the Schlepper – "Milton's a film producer" I said to Patrick.

They shook hands. The Schlepper didn't want to meet another actor either but he did as I slipped away. Was he Milton? No..

****

61

From the high spirits of the production there was only one way to go and that was down and Alfredo went straight down into the black hole of depression despair and paranoia. I received loads of telephone calls from him both at work and home. 'Someone is stealing my oatmeal.' 'Someone is dumping faeces outside my bedroom window.' 'Someone crept into my room one night and turned my light on when I was asleep.' Always someone – some one; he wanted to go to Stinson Beach and commit suicide and he wanted me to drive him there.

I went to see him a few times but he wouldn't let me in. He said he wanted to sleep. He said the landlady was going to send some 'heavies' to see him as he hadn't paid his rent. One time I went to see him he wasn't in and he had put a padlock on his door.

Leah called one of the evenings and asked me where he was. Alfredo had asked me not to tell her so I didn't.

Patrick also called me and wanted his phone number as he said it was time to collect his debt. I didn't give him the number and nor did I give it to Betty who asked for it constantly. I just told them I didn't have it but I knew they didn't believe me.

Alfredo called one time and said that they had padlocked him in and he couldn't get out. He said he had to call for Milton to come and set him free.

I told him that I was going around to see him and that if he didn't let me in I would call the police.

When I got there he was standing on the front door step. He was clean shaven but his skin looked bad. It looked as if he had been scratching his cheeks.

"The landlady is mad at me" he said "for ruining her door."

"Are we going in?" I said.

"Yes. Excuse the place."

His place was no worse than it was before except that the duvet was in a crumpled heap on the futon. I picked it up and spread it out.

"Are you taking your medication?"

"Yes" he said.

"Are you sure?"

"Yes" he said.

"What happened to the *St John's Wort*?"

"I think it was giving me chest pains – I'm back on ZOLOFT. I feel a lot better."

"What about all this business of being locked in?"

"I was locked in. Milton came and got me out."

Who was I to ask – the landlady? I figured Alfredo was in enough internal turmoil without me mixing it with the landlady. He obviously didn't recognize his paranoia.

"Is the Schlepper Milton?"

"The Schlepper? No" he said "Why did you ask that?"

"What's the Schlepper's name?"

"His name – Mark - Mark Ginsberg. Why do you want to know?"

" . . er Patrick wanted to know." It was the first thing that came into my mind.

"Have you been to see the doctor?"

"No."

He sat on the edge of the futon.

"You should see one, you know."

"I'm a lot better now" he said "I just felt so low after the play."

"It was a wonderful evening" I said.

"It was; but it has been downhill ever since."

"Are you working on anything?"

"No" he said.

"Maybe you should start – what about the story of Gertie who travels to the west of Ireland and lives with a group of brothers?"

"I don't know if I'll ever start it. You should write it – you know the story; I've told you enough times."

He stood up.

"Can I get you a cup of tea?"

"Yes please."

He went out and I heard him filling the kettle. Then I heard him walk off.

He didn't tell me where he had put the rest of his things; maybe in the same storage. As far as I know when he left Betty's house no one saw him leave. So if he was helped by the dubiously existing Milton it could not be verified.

I went to his window and looked out to see if I could see where faeces had been dumped. He called it faeces sometimes and sometimes he would simply call it shit. When he needed to go that day he said he wanted to defecate whereas at other times he would use the usual expletives.

After about five minutes I went out to look for him. The kettle was boiling its arse out so I turned it off. Then I saw the bathroom door shut.

"Alfredo?" I called.

Not a word.

"Alfredo?" I knocked the bathroom door.

"Yeh?"

"Come on" I said.

"Won't be long!"

Unbelievable; he couldn't refrain from spending time in the bathroom even for my visit.

I made myself a cup of tea after finding the *Earl Grey* tea bags in the fridge, of all places, next to the jug that Patrick had left him.

I drank the tea and after about twenty minutes he came out of the bathroom.

"Why do you keep your tea bags in the fridge?"

"I have the top shelf for my stuff. They don't use them if I keep them in there but if I keep them in the cupboard they get used."

"You should start to write something" I said.

It was very difficult for us to have a proper conversation. Once in a while I would take a pathetic stab at humour but he wouldn't respond.

I decided to go and leave him to it.

He called me the next day whilst I was at work and told me not to give Leah any knowledge of his whereabouts if she should call again. I started to see Leticia on a regular basis. She was a movie fan so we saw some good films together. Leticia was training to be a nurse and she invited me to meet her family in Guadalajara which, she said, was in a very beautiful part of Mexico. I found that it is quite a common thing for Irish men to marry Mexican women. She had an Irish uncle by marriage and said the two countries were drawn together by a common love of alcohol and a common religion.

A few days after I left Alfredo he called me at the office. It was around seven-thirty in the evening and he wanted to know if I could let him have three dollars and eighty five cents. I asked what he wanted it for and he said it was for something to eat; I knew it was for ice cream. I had four dollars in my pocket; it had been there since I had been at his place. I didn't seem to spend too much since I was driving to work. Petrol was around one dollar a gallon and my mother wouldn't believe it when I told her.

I told Alfredo that he would have to come in and get it and he said he would drive in and pick it up. Twenty minutes or so later I could hear his horn in the car park. He parked right next to the Chevy.

"How's it going?" he said.

"I'm fine."

"No - the car."

"It's going well."

"It'll go forever" he said "you will, eventually, have to shoot it."

He looked a little healthier than he had looked the last time.

"Where are the women?" he said, "where's the pussy?"

He looked up at the office.

"Who's that?" he said.

Christine was sitting in the window and you could see her long hair but not much more than a silhouette.

"Christine." I said.

"Oh: getting a bit big around the arse."

Christine had grown a little bigger in that area but we could hardly see it from the window.

I gave him the four dollars from my pocket. He got back into his car and drove away shouting "coke."

As he drove off I saw him look up again at Christine in the office. He stopped near the exit and blew the horn. I went up to him.

"I wish I could be like you" he said "you're so relaxed; you walk up to people and introduce yourself. I wish I could be like that."

Then he drove off to eat his ice cream and contemplate suicide. When I called my voice mail to check for messages there were two: one from Betty and one from Patrick. They both wanted the same thing – Alfredo's number. I think Betty's message had been there since the morning.

Poor Alfredo: he didn't have two halfpennies to rub together, no company most of the time and those two were hounding him for money. He thought he was a better writer than Harold Pinter – I doubted that – but he had more talent in his little finger than the combined talents of Betty and Patrick so I thought I would let them whistle for their money.

When I got home that night I found Alfredo's lap top computer on my bed. With it was a little note which said 'write about Gertie: love Alf."

Next to it was an instructions booklet.

I walked around the house and nobody was in so nobody could tell me how it got there. The front door was hardly ever locked so he had just come in, dumped the computer on my bed and left. I stood on the porch for a while and I could see the dog next door standing upright, leaning against the fence and wagging its tail; Alfredo had been to say hello and the dog appreciated it.

I called Alfredo's telephone number but there was an official message to say that the line had been disconnected.

Next day I went around to his house and saw the landlady.

"He's gone;" she said "he went last night the poor man. Are you Milton?"

"No" I said "I'm his old room mate."

"He was a tormented soul. I tried to talk to him but he was lost. He gave me his rent last night and went."

"Didn't he give you notice?"

"No but I don't mind. He has enough troubles."

"Did he leave anything behind?"

"Not a thing" she said "everything's gone."

"No forwarding address?"

"No."

About three days later Alfredo called me from somewhere near Stinson Beach.

"Guess where I am?" he said.

I knew straight away where he was and I said "Stinson Beach?"

"Yes" he said "I was there this afternoon."

He sounded content and happy.

"I hope you don't do anything foolish" I said.

"What might be foolish to you might not be foolish" he said.

We didn't say much more, didn't say anything important and it wasn't till we hung up that I realized I hadn't mentioned the computer.

About another week later I received a letter from him in Canada. He told me his car had made it exhaust fumes and all. He was at an address in Vancouver and said that it was no good writing to him that he was leaving that address the following day. I did write to him but he never replied.

62

A few months after Alfredo left I went to Dublin to be with my sister and to see her new baby. It was a he and he was baptised Felix Rufus; another Irishman, I thought at the time, with a name far from being Irish. Maybe he would grow up to be a writer like Alfredo and use his name to confuse his origins.

It was a shock to see my mother when I got back to Dublin. In the time I'd been away she seemed to have aged ten years. She was eighty years of age but the image I had kept in my head whilst I was in Los Angeles was the sprightly mother of a few years previously; the one that used to walk out and play bingo, who would go to mass twice a week and even have a sing-song in the pub once in a while.

She had been confined to a wheel chair, due to arthritis and rheumatism, a few months before my return and nobody had told me; so it was a shock. This was the reason that my sister spent a lot of time at my mother's, when she was pregnant, instead of in her own place.

I had spent a lot of time looking after Alfredo in Los Angeles and there in Dublin was one of my own needing care; she wouldn't let on how ill she had been in case it worried me and made me abandon my new life.

My sister had a new baby to look after so I moved in back home for a while to look after my mother.

I used to take her for a walk through Fairview Park and once in a while I'd wheel her into town. In Los Angeles you could use a wheel chair on the buses but I didn't bother to find out in Dublin. I loved walking around my home town as I missed it no matter how much I loved my new life.

We walked to a few pubs in town and she would sit and drink orange as I would sink the legendary black stuff. Sometimes I would have a few drinks, not enough to be drunk, and I would need to pee a few times "Come on, you bleedin' piss tank" she would say as I would sneak into Fairview Park on the way home.

"Shut up, Mam, will you" I would say and we would laugh.

"Bleedin' piss tank was at it again" she would say to my sister and we would all laugh.

I don't know whether young Felix Rufus picked up any of these words at that very early and tender age but he slept a lot.

Most of the time my mother was confused and suffered from some kind of dementia but she had her good days and I cherished those; I learned a lot about my father and other characters of my family "they were all fond of the gargle" she said one day "they all liked a drop, your father's family and most of them were musicians."

That was something new to me; I had an uncle who would play the mandolin in Roach's pub in Ballybough but that's about all I knew.

On our walks I tried to look for Alfredo. Well not exactly Alfredo himself but some kind of trace that he ever existed. The first thing I did was to look in the telephone directory for Hunter. There were about ten or so and I called each one. No one had heard of Alfredo or even Alfred when I gave them an alternative; one person asked me if I knew who Alfred Hunter was and I answered that I didn't. He said 'Try Ulysses." and hung up.

So Alfred Hunter would be a character in Ulysses; I got a copy of the book and didn't have to look far. Alfred Hunter wasn't in the book at all; he was a person in real life that James Joyce had based Leopold Bloom on. He had come to the service of James Joyce at one time which is why Joyce had used him as a model for Bloom.

So I was back to square one: Alfredo didn't exist in Ireland under that name at all.

I spent some time in Bewley's coffee shop and met someone there that I knew to be a writer who didn't know Alfredo but told me to try McDaids pub which was close by on the corner in Harry Street. "In fact" he said "We'll all go there now and take a look."

I had known McDaids of old and had spent many an hour in there creating a hangover. It attracted writers once in a while but when we got there all we did was drink. After about three or four my mother fell asleep and I decided to take her home. She was still asleep when I got home so I sat in the chair and fell asleep too. When I woke up it was dark and she was sitting by the electric fire looking at the false flames flickering through the cardboard coal effect.

"Why didn't you wake me?" I said.

"You looked quite peaceful so I let you rest. I was just thinking about your father."

I think one of the reasons I liked Alfredo was that he told stories. I missed my father's stories since he was dead as sometimes, when we were young and television hadn't intruded into our lives, both of my parents would tell stories in turn. They would never take part in each other's tales even if they were characters in it. They would tell the stories and we would sit around in the dark in front of a fire of turf. I knew there was a tale coming: we were in the dark and even though the turf fire had been replaced by a cardboard fire effect it reminded me of my Dublin childhood.

"What were you thinking?"

>"About when I met him: We met at McCann's pub. I was outside with Maura Short sheltering from the rain and he came out and told us to move on. He was working in there as a barman. There wasn't a pick on him. He was just like number one."

She held one finger up.

>"He was an awful looking yoke. It was just after I left home. My father was a bastard. Here was I at twenty five and he wanting me in by ten-o-clock. I moved in with Maura Short. They were looking after me.

My father was in the British Army and knew nothing about the Easter uprising - he was away getting gassed. I remember everything about it; the lot. People don't believe me, you know, but I do. I remember the Fourcourts. I think it was the IRA that was in the Fourcourts...think it was...... They came and knocked the door – the British army - and told us not to be frightened of the bomb. Anyway ...my mother said – 'Oh Jesus, Mary and Joseph: you're not going to kill the poor men that's in there?'

They said 'Well if they don't come out - and it's war missus - we'll have to.'

They never came out; they were blown up - and what was left of them put their mate on a stretcher - the door it was a door it was - and they walked down Parnell Street to the Castle. They were singing:

> We fight for Ireland,
>
> Dear Old Ireland
>
> Ireland Boys away."

My mother took a piece of tissue from her sleeve and wiped her eyes:

> "And the British soldiers were all on edge but they never touched them. They carried their oul' comrade - wouldn't let one of them touch them, like you know? I couldn't have lived anywhere else worse than Parnell Street when the nineteen hundred and....when the trouble was on."

She sat there thinking and I could actually see a thought enter her head by the expression on her face; then she laughed.

> "We had - in Parnell Street - it was the one yard for the two houses and it was a door that went through to the yard and over the wall you went and you were at a hill and you were away. Do you know what I mean?"

I did.

> "This bloke was standing at the door - Parnell Street, you know - and another bloke was with him and ran away shouting 'British Bastard' and with that the what-you-call-him? - The Black and Tan followed and, of course, he disappeared over the back. But the Black and Tan came straight up through the houses - never knocked on the door - just opened it. Could be standing there in your nod for all they cared.
>
> They said 'Hello Pop' - of course my grandfather being old with the beard. My father was a British soldier at the time and they thought we were all British. And my father's father had a red white and blue flag hanging through the window; they all stuck flags out. The old bastard was in the British army my father; but he used to come home on leave and go across to the pub with my Uncle Stephen and my Grandfather.
>
> Uncle Tom was posh; he only used to drink wine; port wine. And he used to wear spats on his shoes; he was the posh one of the family. And

if they had have done right with him he would have been a millionaire today - if he'd have lived."

We both laughed at that.

"If he'd have lived he would have been a hundred and forty."

She laughed again and started to cough; I gave her a drink of water. She took a drink and carried on:

"He started a factory. Done a lot of pinching out of the other factory - my Grandfather owned a part share in it - Lymons - and they were starting their own place: Lymons sweet factory in O'Connell Street. My Uncle Tom was to go out and look for orders. Sure my Uncle Stephen drank it all; he couldn't be kept out of the pub. He was in the IRA and went to prison. Uncle Tom went too but they were in different places.

I have such a good memory - people think I'm mad when I tell them things. Grandfather Shea was in the IRA. He was a proper rebel my Grandfather was. But my father and his father were no bleedin' good. They were oul' feckin' British soldiers.

Grandfather Shea was lovely; he used to keep his revolver on the ledge in his room – the room at our house. It was a bit of luck nobody ever found it.

My father used to whip me and Grandfather Shea found out - 'I'll take his bleedin' life...' not bleedin' - they never used bleedin' 'Take his bloody life if you touch her again.' To my father he said that."

She paused again and looked into the cardboard fire.

"We went to live in Marino when I was ten. Our Kathleen was born - she was born in March Kathleen was and she was a new baby when we went to live in Marino. I remember I had one frock on me all day and Kathleen was a baby in my arms. And my whole frock was stained from where she shit - it wasn't shit - it was just the mark.

The one thing my father did for me – the only thing he ever got me during his life - was to buy me a bike – the only thing he ever did - says he 'I'll buy you a bicycle.'

He brought me into a shop on the quay and says he 'Get up and ride it.'
I couldn't ride the bloody thing – I'd told him I could ride a bike. And my father went up and down the alley for to show me how to ride.

Kings End Street was another street where we used to go to learn how to ride the bike. One day we were coming down from Capel Street right down to Parnell Street to Henry Street. There was a private car stood there and didn't I run into the bloody side of the car. All I could hear my father say was 'Get up quick. Come on get up.'

I burst the whole side of the bloody car." She laughed:

"I was the first one in our street to have a bike. But I was never let out to play. The nuns wouldn't let you. You weren't allowed to play in the street.

When my grandfather was the age I am now he lived with us in Marino – one day he had a row with my father. He never liked my father cos my da got my mother into trouble. My Mother was married in August and I was born in the October.

When they had the row my Grandfather got up - he had one of his turns - dying you know - he said 'I'm not going to live here any more' and he got a pair of sticks and he walked up to the entrance, you know, and I kept saying and crying 'Come on home, Granda, come on home;' The poor fella was dying. They could at least have made him feel wanted.

But he wouldn't come home; he wanted Locky - that was the cabman that he latched on to no matter where he was going. No matter where he was going he sent for Locky; he took us to the boat at the North Wall one day when we were going to the Isle of Man for a holiday; me and my grandfather. And he got us on the boat and my grandfather told Locky to come and fetch us and pick us up Friday at a certain time.

Poor oul' grandfather didn't know about having to book lodgings. He couldn't get any; we had to come back."

That was as far as she went that day. On other days she thought she was back with her family in 1922 and sometimes she thought I was my father.

I was still keeping in touch with Leticia and the day I arranged to go back to Los Angeles to see her, my poor old mother died.

****

Epilogue

(A Cold Morning to Die)

Almost seven years later I was searching for something on the internet when I typed 'The Man with the Pen;' up it came by Alfredo Hunter due to open off Broadway the following week. Now was that a coincidence or was that a coincidence? It was on at a theatre in Union Square New York and I knew straight away that I was going to see it. I hadn't been to New York before so this would be my excuse to make the trip.

Oh! By the way I left Betty's house and moved in with Leticia. I had been seeing her on a regular basis and when she finished her nurse's training we decided to get married: another Irishman marrying a Mexican.

I felt the need to go back and live in Ireland and that is where we decided to tie the knot.

Leticia's family travelled over to Dublin and we had a wonderful time at the wedding. As well as her parents, six other relatives made the trip and her best friend was the chief bridesmaid.

We booked a local band to play at the wedding and the Mexicans had the time of their life till the band started to play La Bamba. That was the cue for the Mexicans to go wild; one of them jumped up on the stage and took over the singing. Then another jumped up and persuaded one of the guitarists to lend him his guitar. The tempo of the music went wild and little Felix Rufus's eyes nearly popped out of his head when his mother danced him around the dance floor.

****

But living in Dublin didn't work out. My mother was gone and the Irish were not used to immigrants of colour no matter how light the colour was. It didn't matter how beautiful she was she felt out of place which I didn't like. It might have been her imagination but there is a certain amount of disrespect for Mexicans in Los Angeles and that disrespect Leticia could handle so we decided to go back and live there once again. We got an apartment in Hollywood and I got a job with an internet company out in San Fernando. Leticia carried on nursing and I became quite adept at using the computer.

Somewhere in our apartment was Alfredo's lap top computer and when I saw the item on the internet about his play I looked for it and there it was exactly as he had given it to me.

Maybe I should have tried to write the story he wanted me to write.

I travelled to New York alone and the first thing I noticed on that January morning was how cold it was. I had flown in on the 'red eye' and when I walked out into the fresh air the icy cold hit my face. I was only out in it for about ten seconds as I crossed over to the place where I could get a kind of shuttle train so that I could get the 'A' train into Manhattan.

The 'A' train was full of early morning workers going to work with no smiles on their faces and huddling together on the miserable train; it was a bit of a shock from the bright colours of Los Angeles but it was interesting.

I got off the train at around 14th Street; I had to eat and I knew that it wasn't too far from Union Square where I managed to book a cheap hotel room; again on the internet; Alfredo would be proud.

As soon as I got up the stairs and onto the street I arrived in America. Los Angeles was fun and I loved it but this was America. The buildings were sky high, the steam came out of the drains, yellow cabs screeched by and there were cops all over the place – maybe five or six blue and whites, as they call them; I walked over the street and all the cops had scarves around their faces to keep out the cold; I wished I had. The cold was so bad it hurt my face. The rest of my body seemed to be okay and I found out later that it was one of the coldest winters ever and that the temperature was around zero Fahrenheit; in the words of Bob Dylan I didn't feel so bad after that.

There had been a murder on the subway; a homeless man was sleeping on a bench and this homeless man had a pocket full of money; another homeless man approached him and tried to pick his pocket when the original man pulled a knife and stabbed him. After he was stabbed the victim ran up the stairs and onto the street, pursued by the man with the knife, and then went down some other stairs back down to the subway and died. When I arrived there were bloody foot prints all over the street and I could clearly see the path of the pursuit.

I found a coffee shop around the corner and, whilst I was eating, a couple of cops came in and one said to the other "It's a cold morning to die."

Maybe I would tell Alfredo about it later at the theatre so that he could tell me to write about it: 'write it down' he would say 'you already have the title – A Cold Morning to Die.'

It would be another of the titles he seemed to create like 'The Bloomsday Blackout,' 'The Jew in Tunisia,' "Dog Shit Canyon.'

The theatre in Union Square had a capacity of around one hundred; I know that because I counted the seats. It was the opening night so the place was full and I sat in anticipation; in fact there was a buzz of anticipation about the whole place; the critics were in sitting with their note pads and pens at the ready. I couldn't see Alfredo but I remembered from the Los Angeles public reading that he didn't like coming into the theatre during the show.

A few minutes before curtain up the Schlepper came in and took a seat near the front.

The lights started to fade and eventually faded into black. Big anticipation on my part: there was a lump in my throat and dryness in my mouth. During the black out the music started; it was the same song as before 'Love's Old Sweet Song' but this time it had an eerie quality; it was as if it came from the past. The lights stayed down and then – "Once upon a time, and a long time ago it was, in the city of Dublin, in the land of Ireland, there was a man with a pen." It was my voice; I couldn't believe it. They had kept the tape for all those years and used it. I felt very exposed again. A tear came to my eye; I tried to stop it. I blinked a couple of times and it stopped. I didn't want to miss the show with my own problems as I had at the public reading.

The lights came up and we saw James Joyce in bed. This time it was an Irishman playing Joyce; he was brilliant. He mumbled the beginning which was better than the actor who did it in Los Angeles and really sounded delirious. The woman who played Nora was as good and had a wonderful Galway accent.

When the lights came down for the end of the play there was thunderous applause and people stood up: I stood up too. The two performers looked delighted; they came forward, took their bows and made to go off; but the audience wouldn't let them. People stamped their feet as they clapped their hands then somebody shouted 'author;' then again 'author' 'author;' but there was no author there. Eventually the audience let the performers go and the lights came on.

The play was a masterpiece; at least to my mind it was; maybe it was because I was connected to the play but I felt it was the most exciting time I had ever spent in the theatre. I was sure it was going to be an enormous hit.

Outside I made my way to the Schlepper; at first he didn't recognize me, but then he said "I tried to get hold of you for permission to use your voice."

"That's okay" I said.

"I'll get you to sign a paper – you'll get paid."

"Sure" I said "Where's Alfredo?"

"He has an agent in London who collects his royalties – that's all I know."

"You haven't seen him since Los Angeles?" I said.

"No - everything was done through his London agent. He doesn't write any more. It's too painful for him. He said he wanted to be a bum with no responsibility; said he wanted to sleep under the stars down the subway and like that. The guy's nuts: with this he has it made."

"He's not sleeping in the subway in New York is he?"

I thought about the bum in the subway murder that morning.

"No he's not here; he's in Ireland. I just don't know where."

When I got back to Los Angeles I told Leticia about my trip; she could see that I had been through an emotional experience and had been inspired. I took the lap top computer and put it onto my desk and set my mind to the fact that I would be writing the story Alfredo had wanted me to write; the story of the girl going to the west coast of Ireland in search of a husband; the story he had told me about over and over again - I would have to think about it, of course and maybe look at the stars like Alfredo did; or maybe as Alfredo was still doing in what part of Ireland I knew not.

We didn't have a garden where we lived in Hollywood and because of the bright city lights my view of the heavens was not as good as the view we used to have from Silverlake which was only around ten miles away.

I went out onto the balcony and looked up; it was around nine in the evening in that part of America which meant it was five in the morning all over Ireland. At that time of the year it would be night in both places. I could see the moon and if it was a clear sky in Ireland the people there would be able to see the same moon if they were up early enough.

It was too early for Pickard the sheep shagger to pass our house and ignore the door he used to knock; but it was never too early for Alfredo or even too late for him to look at the stars. Leticia had confirmed to me that she was pregnant so maybe there was a little Alfredo on the way and maybe a story I could write. Maybe Alfredo was still staring at the stars as I stood staring; still wondering if I could maybe be a storyteller too; maybe!

*